BUTLER RANCH *Christmas*

USA TODAY BESTSELLING AUTHOR

HEATHER SLADE

Table of Contents

1

Laird

There would be no Christmas lights strung on Butler Ranch's main residence this year, at least by me. Perhaps one of our children would take on the task. However, they'd spent nearly every day of the last three at the hospital, visiting their mother, just like I had.

I suppose if we got word that my beloved wife would be able to come home for the holiday, we'd have to get right to it, or there'd be certain hell to pay.

Sorcha Steward Butler—or Rua, as I'd first known her—was a formidable force of nature. While I'd never dare call her spoiled or even think of her that way, she wasn't known to be shy about wanting things her way.

These were the kinds of thoughts I forced my brain to have rather than allow my mind to drift to the black abyss my life would become without her. The idea alone brought an unbearable ache to my chest.

1

Ainsley

One year ago

"When are you leaving for Christmas break?" asked Bryn.

I bit my lower lip. "I'm not sure. What about you?"

"I don't know either, but I can tell you I'm not too excited about it. I'm thinking about coming back on the twenty-sixth. I'd drive home Christmas night if I didn't think my mother would have a stroke." Bryn was my friend, former roommate, and colleague in the research department at Stanford's Graduate School of Business.

"Why?"

"Seriously?"

"What?"

She folded her arms. "You don't remember that when I came back from Thanksgiving break, I told you Greg is engaged?"

"Sorry. Um, yeah, I remember." I was too caught up in my own relationship drama to think about Bryn's high school boyfriend's engagement announcement.

"Too bad we can't go home together."

"Right." How would that work? Bryn's family lived in Mendocino, which was in the opposite direction of where my parents did.

"What's going on with you and Cris?"

I was less sure of that than I was about when I'd head home.

As much as I'd hoped I would, I hadn't seen or talked to Cristobal Avila since I left for my brother Brodie's wedding, which took place on Thanksgiving Day.

"I want to spend the holidays with you," he'd said when we talked about our plans. "I'm done hiding our relationship. My sister is marrying your brother on Christmas Eve."

It'd been hard to believe that by the end of the year, all three of my brothers would be married or that, two months ago, they'd all been single. There were times I'd doubted any of them would ever marry.

"Ainsley? Are you listening to me?" Cris had asked me.

"I'm not sure the timing is right to tell our families about our relationship."

"For God's sake, we've lived together for *six years*."

Cris and I had grown up next door to each other. Sort of. Both our parents owned ranches on the Central Coast of California in Paso Robles' wine country. Given acres of land separated our houses, it wasn't like we could've waved at each other. Not that we would've. The relationship between our two families was almost as bad as the Hatfields and McCoys.

Cris blindsided me that night by giving me an ultimatum. Either he and I went home—and to the wedding—as a couple, or we were finished.

I'd left Stanford the following Monday with every intention to talk to Brodie and ask if I could bring Cris with me. Instead, I'd chickened out.

When he called later that night to see how the conversation went, I stalled. "The wedding isn't until Friday. I'll talk to him tomorrow."

"That's it, Ainsley. I can't do this anymore."

He'd hung up then, and when I tried to call him back, he didn't answer. I'd called again and texted, but he never responded. When I got back the following Monday, he'd moved all his stuff out of our apartment.

Part of me had hoped he'd show up at Brodie's wedding anyway, surprising my family and me. But he hadn't. He'd left it to me, and I hadn't had the courage to tell our families I was in love with him. If I had, someone might have asked how long I had been. Honestly, it was since I was nine years old.

The day before Cris left home at eighteen to begin his journey in medicine at Stanford, I went looking for him. At first I thought he hadn't noticed me watching him from high in a tree near the split-rail fence that divided my family's property from his.

"What are you doing up there, little one?" he shouted.

"I came to say goodbye."

"How do you know I'm leaving?"

"Alex said you were." I hoped he wouldn't ask when I'd talked to his sister, since I'd been spying on her and my brother at the time.

"I'm glad I took a walk out this way today, then."

I scrambled to climb out of the tree, but slipped and fell instead. Cris raced over and checked my arms and legs to make sure I hadn't broken anything.

"You'll be a good doctor someday."

He'd smiled and ruffled my hair and, for a split second, touched my cheek with his fingertip. I knew then that I'd love Cristobal Avila forever.

The next time I saw him, I was eighteen myself. I recognized him right away when I saw him walk across the main quad of the farm—known to most as Stanford University. He was impossible to miss, given he was the most beautiful man I'd ever seen.

"Hey, there," I said when he walked past. "I was hoping I'd run into you."

"Um…hi. Do I know you?"

It was like someone had popped my balloon when he didn't recognize me. The bravado I'd felt when I said hello was gone, leaving me feeling horribly embarrassed.

"Hey, Cris." My older sister walked up behind him and handed me a cup of coffee.

"Hey, Skye. Wait." He looked at me a second time. "Ainsley? What are you doing here?"

"Orientation. It's always been her dream to attend Stanford," Skye answered before I could.

"Yep," I said, rolling my eyes, more embarrassed than I had been, if that was possible. "My dream come true," I muttered.

I wanted to kick Skye when she added, "It was Stanford or nowhere."

"Well, wow. This is great. It's nice to see someone from home."

"Are you a doctor yet?" Skye asked.

"Yep. Second year of residency at Stanford Medical Center. What are you here for, Ainsley?"

You, I wanted to answer. "Business," I said instead.

"It's a tough school to get into. Congratulations."

When he leveled his perfect smile at me, his two dimples creased his face, and I swooned. I longed to run my fingers through his thick, inky, perfectly unkempt hair and my lips over the stubble that made him look as rugged as he was handsome.

"Thanks," I mumbled, trying to look anywhere but at him. I couldn't, though. He was magnetic.

"She's a brainiac," said Skye. "Kind of like you. I don't know where she gets it from. No one else in our family is."

"I'm sure that isn't true, Skye," Cris said, looking at me in a panty-dropping way. When his gaze left me and settled on his watch, my heart dropped.

"I gotta go, or I'll be late, but again, it was really good to run into you. Let's get together when I have more time. Maybe we can even carpool home sometime."

"I'd love that."

"Soon," he'd said, waving as he hurriedly walked away.

Soon turned into three years. We never carpooled home. Not once. And as hard as I'd tried to, I'd only gotten close enough to speak to him once between then and my twenty-first birthday.

I was walking up the stairs of the Stanford Clinic and saw him a few steps ahead, in the empty stairwell. When he reached the landing, he looked right at me. I raised my arm to wave, but Cris looked away. "I can't do this," I thought I heard him mutter.

After that, I stopped looking for him. I didn't need more humiliation. Even if I had seen him, I would've walked in the opposite direction.

The night of my twenty-first birthday, my room-mates and best friends, Gwen and Bryn, took me out to—in their words—get me drunk. It wasn't as though I'd never had alcohol before; my family owned a winery, for goodness' sake.

We ended up at Antonio's Nut House on California Avenue in Palo Alto, where Grateful Dead music played loudly and there was an endless supply of peanuts to eat. The place was known for cheap drinks, billiards, retro arcade games, and decent Mexican food in its adjoining restaurant.

Given I was usually the designated driver, I was stunned when not one, but three shot glasses appeared in front of me along with my third or fourth pint of beer. I'd lost count.

"The Fireball is from me," said Gwen. "The Scotch Whiskey is from Bryn, and the shot of tequila is from this handsome man I found sitting at the bar. He says he knows you. Is this true, Ains? Have you been holding out on us?"

Gwen's gaze traveled up and down the length of Cristobal Avila's body, whose eyes met mine.

"Come on, then. Line 'em up." Gwen held up her shot glass and waited for me to do the same.

The Fireball burned as it slid down my throat, and the thought of having two more shots made me nauseous.

"My turn." Bryn pushed in front of Gwen. "I want a full report tomorrow," she said, looking over her shoulder. "He's so hot," she mouthed, raising her glass. "*Sláinte*, my friend."

"Bathroom break," Gwen shouted after she and Bryn downed their whiskey. I stood to join them even though I didn't need to go.

"Not you," said Bryn, who pushed me back down on the barstool and walked away.

"It's your birthday." Cris leaned close enough to kiss my cheek, but I shrugged away. He smiled and rested his arm on the table.

"It's my turn," he said. "I've been waiting a long time for this."

I closed my lids and shook my head. Had he really just said he'd waited a long time to do a shot with me, or was I imagining things in my alcohol-addled state? I took a sip of beer and looked into his mossy-green eyes.

He brushed the hair away from my face and leaned forward again. "Happy birthday, Ainsley."

I thought about the day in the stairwell. Why was he being nice to me now, when then, he wouldn't even say hello?

"Are you sure you want to do this?" he asked.

His lips almost touched mine. Was he asking if I wanted to kiss him? *Absolutely.* I wanted to do that all night long, but no, I couldn't. I closed my eyes again, shook my head, and heard him laugh.

Oh, God—I was a joke to him. I grabbed my purse and tried to push past him, but he snaked his arm around my waist.

"Where are you going?" His mouth was close enough to my ear that I could hear him whisper even though the bar was packed with people.

"I have to go." I had to get away from him before I made an even bigger fool of myself or had more to drink, in which case, I'd turn into a full-blown idiot.

"I meant the shot," he said. "Are you sure you want another one?"

I tried to wriggle away, but Cris tightened his grip.

"Ainsley Butler," he breathed. "You're all grown up now. And just as beautiful as I knew you'd be."

He was drunk. He had to be. Or I was dreaming. That was more likely. Cris Avila had completely forgotten

I was at Stanford and that he'd told me he'd see me soon—three years ago. Except for that one time when he'd intentionally ignored me.

He took my purse off my arm, set it on the table, and handed me the shot glass. When he lifted it to his lips and tossed it back, I did too, disregarding the lemon slices and salt sitting on the table.

I weaved a little and sat on the stool. I closed my eyes, but that didn't help. In fact, it made the vertigo worse.

"Come on," he said, taking my hand. "Let's get you out of here."

I jerked out of his grasp. "I'm not going anywhere with you…You…ignored me."

Cris sat on the stool next to me and ran his hand through his hair.

"I'm sorry," I saw him mouth.

"Why?"

He studied me, focusing on my lips.

"I know you saw me."

We sat that way, staring at each other, for what felt like a long time. Neither of us spoke. Finally, Cris took a deep breath and then let it out. "Do you know how old I am, Ainsley?"

I took another sip of beer, then another, even though more alcohol was the last thing I needed. "What did you mean before, when you said you'd been waiting a long time for this?"

He shook his head and turned away.

"Forget it." I grabbed my purse and wound my way through the crowded bar, looking for Gwen and Bryn.

After searching everywhere and not seeing them, I went to the ladies' room. I stood in the long line of women waiting outside the door until the vertigo got bad enough that I had to sit.

I found a bench, plopped down on it, and covered my face with my hands.

I closed my eyes tight, wishing I knew where my friends were. They wouldn't have just left me here, would they?

I felt a hand touch my hair, and when I opened my eyes, Cris was crouched down in front of me.

"Are you okay?"

"I'm fine." I leaned away from his hand that was still stroking my hair.

"I don't think you are."

I tried to stand, but he had me caged between him and the bench.

"Why are you here? Why tonight?" When my eyes filled with tears, I cursed the alcohol for making me so emotional. "Please, just go. Leave me alone. Haven't you humiliated me enough?"

He shook his head. "I can't do that."

"You can." I pointed in the direction of the front door. "Just go."

"I never meant to humiliate you, *niña bonita.* I had to stay away from you."

"W-w-w-h-y?" I full-on cried, only adding to my embarrassment.

He tweaked my nose, making me feel like I was nine years old again.

"Our families…"

Yes, I knew our families were enemies, but wasn't that between our fathers? Alex and Maddox had been together forever, but that wasn't a good argument since, even though almost everyone knew about them, they still kept their relationship a secret.

"You spoke to Skye when she brought me for orientation."

He nodded.

"Why can you talk to her and not me?"

"Because I never wanted to kiss Skye." Cristobal held me still with the hand he'd woven into my hair and kissed me.

At first he was tentative and sweet, but then he pushed his tongue between my lips and into my mouth. I could taste lingering tequila and licked his bottom lip. When I did, he kissed me harder.

"Oh, oops!"

I looked up and saw Bryn. Gwen was behind her. "I've been looking for you. Where were you?" I asked, hating how much I sounded like a little girl.

"Mm-hmm." Gwen stood, hands on her hips, looking at Cris, whose hand was still woven in my hair.

"We're on our way to the Stube," said Bryn, looking at Cris as well. "Wanna come with us?"

Instead of answering my friend, he looked at me.

"Go." I pushed him away, and he let go of my hair. "I'm going home."

"Come on, Ains," Gwen pleaded. "It's your birthday; we're supposed to be celebrating."

"I don't feel like celebrating." I crossed my arms and hoped I was being a big enough bitch that he'd just leave.

"I'll make sure Ainsley gets home okay. I don't think she needs anything more to drink," Cris said to Gwen and Bryn as though I wasn't there.

"Hey!" I swatted him. "First of all, I'm right here and can hear you. Second, I can make my own decisions about whether I've had enough to drink or not." I glared at the grinning man.

"If you're sure…" Gwen said, and Cris nodded.

My friends were leaving without me? Seriously?

He grasped my hand. "Come on, *niña bonita*. I'll take you home."

"But…but…"

Bryn walked away, waving and blowing a kiss.

"See you tomorrow," said Gwen, waving too.

I followed Cris, knowing that as soon as I got out of the overly warm bar and breathed some fresh air, I would feel better. Then I'd tell Cris I could find my own way back to the apartment I shared with my two so-called friends who had just deserted me.

When we got outside, Cris whistled so loud it hurt my ears.

"Sorry," he said when he saw me wince. "It's the only way to get a cab on a Friday night."

Instead of feeling better as we stood waiting, I felt woozier. I grabbed Cristobal's sleeve to steady myself.

"Come here," he said, tucking me under his arm.

"Where to, lovebirds?" the taxi driver asked when he met us at the curb.

"Twelve Beacon Way," he said and helped me into the backseat.

"Where are we going?" I asked when the car began moving.

"My apartment."

"No, I can't do that. I have to go home."

A wave of wooziness hit me again, but this time it felt like I was going to be sick. "Um, please pull over. *Hurry.*" The driver crossed two lanes of traffic and came to a screeching stop.

I made it out of the cab in the nick of time, losing the contents of my stomach in a nearby shrub. Cris had gotten out too. He stood beside me, rubbing my back as waves of nausea reverberated through me.

"My apartment is around the corner," he said once my heaving subsided. "Come on."

I wiped my mouth with the back of my hand. "Okay, but then you have to take me home. I mean my home."

When I woke the next morning, my head felt fuzzy, but I wasn't nearly as hungover as I'd expected I would be.

I opened my eyes, looked around, and cringed. On top of what I assumed was his bed lay a fully clothed but sound asleep Cristobal Avila. Thankfully, I was fully clothed, too.

His eyes opened, and he caught me staring.

"How do you feel this morning?" he asked.

"Better than expected. I guess I didn't have as much to drink as I thought."

"No, you did. Three shots on an empty stomach, plus beer—that's a lot."

"How did you know I had an empty stomach?"

"I guess you don't remember begging me to go get us a couple of burgers last night."

I gasped and brought my hand to my mouth. "Oh, God, did I really? I'm sorry."

"Don't be. I didn't go."

"Thank goodness."

"I had them delivered."

I brought the pillow to my face and groaned. "I'm so mortified."

"Hey. Look at me."

I gazed into his perfect eyes.

"It's okay, Ainsley. I feel at least half responsible for how inebriated you got last night, which was only one of the reasons I wanted you to stay here—so I could look after you."

"What was the other reason?"

"Are you sure you want me to answer that?"

I nodded.

"I'll tell you over breakfast."

2

Cristobal

It had taken two shots of tequila for me to leave the bar where I met friends for drinks after a long and grueling day at the medical center and walk next door to the place where I knew Ainsley Butler would be celebrating her twenty-first birthday.

No matter how often I told myself that the nine-year age difference between us was too much, every time I saw her around campus, I felt the same magnetic pull I had the day she showed up at the farm with her older sister.

When I ran into one of her roommates early the day of her birthday and she told me where they'd be that night, I knew that against my better judgment, I'd show up too.

That was six years ago, and in that time, I'd fallen more and more in love with the red-haired, blue-eyed force of nature.

Ainsley was smart—brilliant, really—beautiful, funny, kind, loving, and sexy as shit. Playing connect the dots with the freckles scattered all over her body was my favorite pastime.

But we had a big problem. No one in either of our families knew we were together, and from what I could tell, Ainsley wanted to keep it that way as long as possible. I was beginning to think she'd *never* be willing to take our relationship public.

Was it the difference in our ages that made me impatient? I loved Ainsley. I could see us spending our lives together. Maybe she just wasn't there yet.

I'd recently moved from a traditional medical practice into genetic research. By doing so, I was challenged professionally in a way I never had been, working in a hospital. My income was significantly more and my hours regular.

Ainsley, on the other hand, was just about to finish her PhD. Maybe once she had, her line of thinking would be closer to mine.

We'd always been so in sync, from the first weekend we spent together. We both took our studies seriously and excelled in our chosen programs. Neither of us liked to go out all that much. We were happy just staying at home, spending time together.

Physically, no one had ever come close to turning me on the way Ainsley did.

I shook my head and stared up at the ceiling of the studio apartment I'd rented in a spur of the moment when I gave her an ultimatum and the outcome didn't go the way I'd wanted it to.

Now here I was—alone—missing the one person I wanted to spend time with more than any other. I craved her smile, her laugh, and her conversation as much as I craved her body.

What was wrong with me? Had I really believed that someone like Ainsley would respond to an ultimatum? And if she had, would that have made me feel better about our relationship, or would I have felt like I'd pushed her into doing something she wasn't ready to do?

Before I could talk myself out of it, I grabbed my keys and drove to the place I knew she'd be.

3

Ainsley

"Yoo-hoo, Ainsley?" Bryn waved her hand in front of my face. "Are you listening?"

"Sorry. Uh…what?"

"I was telling you I really didn't want to go home for Christmas…never mind. There's someone here to see you."

I'd been working on a presentation comparing organizational structures and how each affected productivity levels, but as usual, my thoughts kept drifting to Cris.

"What is up with you?" Bryn stood and put her hands on her hips, but before I could respond, she walked out of my office. "Never mind, I'll let him in," I heard her mutter.

The Kensey Management Center was locked up tight on Saturdays. Only faculty, PhD candidates, and graduate students had key cards that worked on the weekend. Everyone else had to be buzzed in by someone with proper credentials.

I didn't remember expecting anyone but opened my calendar anyway to check.

When I looked up to ask Bryn who it was, Cris was standing in my doorway.

He didn't walk into my office; he bounded. By the time I rose from my chair, he was standing so close I could feel the warmth of his breath. He laced his hands with mine and leaned forward so our foreheads touched.

"I've missed you so much," he whispered. He dropped one of my hands so he could move the hair from my neck and nipped at the spot where my shoulder curved.

I breathed in the musky scent of his maleness, and every part of my body tuned into him, despite how my brain screamed that we needed to talk. He was so close that all I had to do was turn my head and I could kiss him.

Instead, my knees went soft and I clung to him as his lips trailed from my neck, up to the curve of my cheek, and finally, thankfully, to my lips.

He lifted me so my bottom rested on my desk and angled his neck so his mouth could ravish mine. It was never just a kiss with Cris; it was a full assault on every one of my senses. I slid my hands inside his jacket and clawed at his chest through his shirt.

He was the first to pull back, resting his forehead against mine again while we both caught our breath.

"I need to be alone with you, Ains." He took my hand and led me out of my office, turning off the lights and closing the door behind us. With my fingers laced with his, I followed him to the elevator.

When the door opened on the first floor, I saw Cris had parked his Tesla in the loading zone, not that he would've been ticketed on a Saturday. He knew this, even though he wasn't at Stanford anymore.

My place, which used to be his place, was closer, and I knew that's where he was headed. He parked in my designated spot, since my car was still at the Kensey building, got out, and came around to open my door.

I rummaged through my bag before remembering I'd left my key in the desk drawer.

"I have mine." Cris took his keys out of his pocket and opened the door, waving me through it.

Once inside, I shrugged my jacket off and threw it on the back of the dining room chair.

"Come with me." Cris held out his hand and led me into the bedroom, nuzzling my neck with full lips too perfect to be bestowed on a man.

It wasn't just his lips; everything about him was beautiful. He'd tell me how he loved staring into my bright-blue eyes, but his mossy-green ones, with flecks of cinnamon and gold, turned my brain to putty.

"Let your hair down, Ains," he whispered, removing the clip that held the long, untamable strands of muted-pumpkin-colored hair that hung down past my waist. Each time I'd threaten to trim its length, Cris talked me out of it.

"You're wearing too many clothes," he said, grasping the bottom of my sweatshirt and easing it over my head while I focused on shimmying out of the yoga pants I'd worn to the office, thinking no one besides Bryn would see me today.

When my clothes were off, I watched as Cris reached behind him and pulled his shirt over his head, baring the hardness of his torso. I ran my hands over his flawless skin while he unfastened his belt, then his jeans, letting them fall to the floor along with his boxer briefs.

We lay on the bed, rolling so he covered my body with his. He licked the tip of his finger and ran the pad of it over my plump bottom lip, then scattered kisses on my neck, trailing them down my body with his tongue.

"Ainsley. Sweet Ainsley."

I shivered under his touch.

"Do you know how much I love you? It's why I don't want to hide anymore."

My body arched to his, but I couldn't marry his words with the way his hands and mouth tormented me.

"Wait." I rested my palms on his shoulders and squeezed. "Stop, Cris."

He looked into my eyes and stilled.

"I don't want to hide anymore either," I said, running my fingers through the natural curls of his hair.

Cris turned his head and rested his cheek against my belly. "Are you sure?"

I nodded. "It's time. I'm ready."

We made love for hours, satiating our bodies and reconnecting our souls. We talked and laughed and ordered food, comfortably eating it in nothing but our skin. I loved Cristobal Avila, and it was time my family knew it.

He put my bags in the back of his car and held my door open. "I have to stop and pick up my tux."

I nodded. My bridesmaid's dress was already at my parents' house. I'd picked it up the same day I got the dress I wore for Brodie's wedding.

My brother Maddox and Cris' sister, Alex, had kept their relationship a secret, although not a very closely guarded one. When they announced their engagement, no one seemed surprised.

Would it be the same for us? Maddox and Alex had been together for twenty years before they "came out" to our families. We'd been together six, and the whole time, we'd hidden our relationship like they had. We'd never spent holidays together, even going as far as driving separate cars when we visited Paso Robles at the same time. The biggest difference, though, was that we'd been living together the whole time. Somehow, that seemed worse.

Later today, our families would know we'd been lying to them. While I wasn't ready to face the consequences, losing Cristobal would be far worse.

"We'll go to Los Cab and talk to Alex first," Cris said once we'd made the turn onto Adelaida Trail.

I agreed with that approach. If we told his sister first and she was on our side, she'd get everyone else to fall in line. That hinged on Alex being at her family's place instead of at Butler Ranch, though.

Cris reached over and held my hand. "I called and asked her to meet me there," he said, as though he could read my mind.

"That's good." I looked out the window at the vineyards that had been planted in these fields longer than I'd been alive. They never changed, even when it felt like everything in my life was.

It wasn't just that my brothers were getting married; two of them were also moving away from Butler Ranch, where they'd lived all their lives.

My life with Cris was changing too, whether we told our families about us or not.

A few months ago, he'd left his position as a staff physician at Stanford Medical Center to become the chief medical officer for Geneco, a research-based corporation whose mission was to understand and influence the genetic basis of aging. While the company was based in Palo Alto, Stanford had made him sign the lease on his campus apartment over to me.

When I came back from Brodie's wedding, though, he'd moved all his stuff out. This morning was the first time I saw the studio apartment he'd been living in since our breakup.

It dawned on me that Cris had said *me*. "Does Alex know I'll be with you?"

"What do you mean?"

"You said 'me,' not 'us.'"

"If I had asked my sister to meet both of us at Los Cab, don't you think she would've asked why? You know Alex; she would've been like a dog with a bone." Cris squeezed my hand. "This was my idea. Remember? I'm the one who's been pushing for us to come clean."

Come clean? Like what we'd been doing was dirty?

"Stop it." Cris' tone came out harsh, but when I turned to look at him, he was smiling. "Ainsley, please."

"Please, what?"

"You're an adult, and so am I. Why do you think anyone will even care when they find out we're together?"

"We've talked about this."

"You've talked. I've disagreed."

That made me smile. Every time we'd argued about "coming clean," as he put it, he'd disagreed with what he called my "paranoia."

"It's going to be fine, Ains. Trust me." He squeezed my hand again. "Close your eyes and meditate for a few minutes."

"Thanks, Doc." It was typical advice from Doctor Alternative-Medicine-Balance-Your-Chi Avila. He was all about things like acupuncture, cupping, and meditation, not as a replacement for traditional medicine, but definitely as an enhancement.

Cris believed people could, one day, live to be five hundred or even older. All he needed to do was figure out the science, or guide his research team to figure it out. He wasn't the only one who believed it was possible. Even before Geneco finalized their initial operating plan, they'd been given five hundred million dollars by a venture capitalist firm.

He brought my hand to his lips and kissed each of my fingertips. "Relax, baby. You're wound so tight."

I rolled my shoulders, trying to work out the tension that had settled there.

"There you go," he coaxed. The man had an arsenal of relaxation methodologies. Some I preferred more than others, mainly the ones that required both of us to be naked and touching each other's bodies. If only we could have some time alone before going to his mother's house or to my parents'.

"Cris, where are we staying?"

"I'm not sure yet, but it will work itself out." Instead of just my fingers, Cris brought my palm to his mouth and kissed it as though he was kissing my lips.

"You better sort it out if you intend to keep doing things like that with your tongue."

The smoldering look on his face almost made me ask if we could skip our visit to Los Cab and find a hotel room in town. That would start an argument, though. Cris would say I was trying to delay what we'd both agreed to do today, and he'd be right.

"She's here," he said almost absentmindedly but distinctly relieved.

"Were you worried she wouldn't be?"

He shook his head. "I'm just glad she wasn't late."

4

Ainsley

When we drove up in front of the house Cris grew up in and where his mother now lived alone, I realized I'd never been inside of it.

Cris parked in the circular drive and came around to open my door. When I climbed out, Alex was waiting on the porch.

"Hoo-wee," she shouted, walking around the Tesla. "That car is almost as pretty as the woman riding in it." Alex walked over to hug me. "How are you, girlfriend?"

"I'm good, thanks. How are you? Maddox driving you crazy yet?"

"Your brother has been driving me crazy for a couple decades, Ainsley." Alex laughed. "But about the wedding, no. He's been great."

"Put me to work now that I'm finally here. What can your slacker bridesmaid do to help?"

Cris put his arm around my shoulders.

"Day-um, you two look good together." Alex slugged Cristobal. "How come you've never asked this pretty girl out? She's been living right under your nose for…how long? I've lost track. Ainsley, how long have you been at Stanford now?"

"Uh…nine years," I mumbled, stealing a quick glance at Cris. I could feel the heat spread from my neck up to my face. There was nothing I could do to stop it. When I was embarrassed, the world knew it.

Cris kissed my forehead. "Good idea, Al. Maybe I should do that."

"Oh…my…God." Alex put her hand over her mouth. "This is why we never see you two together. It's so obvious."

"Thought it was about time Ains and I came out of the closet, so to speak."

"About time?" Alex turned to me. "How long has it been?"

"Six years," Cris answered. Was it my imagination, or did his chest puff out a little?

I wanted to crawl back in Cris' car and rewind the last twenty minutes. In my time-travel version, I'd have him drop me off at Butler Ranch before coming to Los Cab.

"I'm the first person you've told."

It wasn't a question, but Cris and I nodded anyway. Alex rubbed her hands together.

"This is going to be fun. And I'm glad you picked me. I mean, it's obvious why you did. Who's gonna say a word about you keeping this a secret from me— the queen of secret relationships." Alex pulled me by the hand toward the front door. "Come on, let's go tell Mama." We found her in the kitchen.

"Mama, you know Ainsley Butler, right?"

"Of course I do." She dropped the spoon she'd been using to stir something on the stove, wiped her hands on her apron, and gathered me in a hug before stepping back and looking into my eyes. "It's good to see you, sweetheart."

I tried to blink away my threatening tears. Cris' mom was being so nice to me, and all this time, I'd been the one refusing to tell everyone the truth. No wonder he'd threatened to break things off with me. "Thank you, Mrs. Avila."

"What's this? Why are you crying? And please, call me Lucia."

I shook my head, knowing if I said anything else, I'd cry harder. Lucia reached behind her and picked up a wooden spoon from the counter. She whacked Cris with it.

"Ow! What was that for?" he exclaimed.

"This is the first time you brought this beautiful girl to see your mama? What's wrong with you?"

When Alex started to laugh, I did too. Cris, though, looked baffled.

"I hope everyone reacts the way you both have," I said, nudging him.

Lucia took my hand and led me to a chair by the kitchen table. "Sit. I want to talk to you."

When Alex and Cris followed, Lucia shooed them off. "I want to talk to Ainsley alone. Go on, now."

Alex shrugged at Cris, but they both left the kitchen.

"Listen to me. Are you listening?"

I nodded.

"The past is long gone, *mija*. God rest my Alfonso's soul, but what he did to our families…" She shook her head. "Such an awful waste."

"Thank you, Mrs. Avila. My father was just as much to blame, though."

"Lucia. Or Mama. Either will work fine for me. Although Sorcha…well, that's okay. You call her Ma, no?"

I smiled and nodded.

"Anyway, I don't think your father would've let it go on so long."

"I don't know…"

Lucia patted my hand. "He's quite a catch, my Cristobal. But he is the one who has gotten the better prize."

"Thank you." I felt my cheeks heating again, but at least I'd stopped crying.

"Do you love him?"

"I do. Very much."

"Good. Because he loves you more. A lot more."

"How do you know that?" I didn't doubt Cris loved me, but I was curious why Lucia was so convinced he loved me more than I loved him.

"A *madre* knows, *mija*. Wait until you tell Sorcha. She'll say the same thing as me."

"I'm not worried about my parents as much as…"

"Ah, your brothers." Lucia stood and put her hands on her hips. "All I can say is your timing is very, very good."

"Why's that?"

"Because they're all so in love." Lucia rolled her eyes and twirled her index finger in the air. "They're crazy with it."

We both laughed.

Alex stuck her head inside the kitchen. "What's going on in here?"

Lucia pointed at her. "She's *loca*, too. Everybody is these days. No weddings for a hundred years, and everybody gets married in a month."

"It's more than a month, Mama."

Lucia's eyes got wide when Cris stuck his head in the door too. "Wait—is there another wedding?"

"No…no," I stammered. "It's just that we…you know…with Maddox and Alex…and both of us…in the wedding."

Lucia elbowed Alex. "You make sure she catches the bouquet, yes?"

"You don't have to go with us," Cris told his sister when she walked us out to his car.

"First of all, I was going there anyway. And second, I'm not going with you; you're following me." Alex snatched Cris' key fob from his hand. "Mine are in the car." She pointed to her BMW parked not too far from the Tesla.

"Uh, no," Cris protested, but Alex laughed.

"It's only a couple miles. What can I do to it in a couple miles?"

Cris glared at her and approached me. He held both my hands in his and looked into my eyes. "This one will be harder on me than you, Ains."

"We don't—"

He kissed me as if he sensed I was going to tell him we didn't have to do this now. I agreed it would be best to just get it over with, though.

What I thought was a kiss to shut me up turned into something so much more when Cris backed me up against his car. What the man could do with his lips and tongue. If Alex weren't watching us, I would wrap my legs around his waist and let him ravish me all he wanted.

"Thank you, Ainsley. I know this wasn't easy for you. It means a lot to me that you're doing this."

"I love you, Cris."

"Not as much as I love you. Not even close."

"Your mother just said that."

"How could I not, Ains. Just look at yourself. You're the most beautiful woman in the valley. Maybe even in the universe. You're smart, you're funny, and you can definitely hold your own with my sister." Cris leaned down to look at Alex, who was smiling at him from the driver's seat. "And nobody else can do that."

"She's a Butler. All of 'em got it over me," Alex quipped. "Let's go, girlfriend. I gotta drive this Tesla. How much did you pay for this baby, anyway?"

Cris shook his head and smiled. "About three times what you paid for yours."

When Alex got to the end of the driveway, she turned right instead of left on Adelaida Trail, going in the opposite direction of my parents' place.

"You know he's never gonna let me drive this again. I gotta get as much playtime in as I can." Alex sped out to the highway. "It'll be okay, you know. Like I said, no one is going to say a word, even your brothers. What can they say? Anything they try—well, you could just cut 'em off by tossin' it over to Maddox."

"I feel like it's different."

"How?"

"Maddox didn't lie."

"And you did?"

I thought about it for a minute. I hadn't lied either, except by omission, which Maddox had done too. "I guess you're right."

"The only difference is that you and Cris were in Palo Alto, and Mad and I sowed our oats at home, where everyone could see us."

Alex turned on Vineyard Road and, once she was away from the traffic on the highway, opened up the car again. "Hey, uh, do I have to worry about juice? I mean, am I using all the battery?"

I shrugged. "I have no idea. I've never driven it."

"What? We'll remedy that right now."

I drove the Tesla up in front of my parents' house and saw Maddox, Naughton, and Cris sitting on the porch. Each had a glass of wine and a cigar.

"What's the occasion?"

"Brodie just called—"

"What?" Alex exclaimed. "Oh my God, Peyton hasn't had the baby yet, has she? I'm supposed to be there."

I knew I hadn't been alone, the day of their wedding, thinking the woman who was now Brodie's wife looked like she was ready to go into labor any minute, and that was over a month ago.

Maddox walked over and put his arm around her. "He called less than two minutes ago and said he'd left you a voicemail."

Alex took her phone out and looked at the screen. "Oh, thank God. Okay, I gotta run." She looked at me. "You're gonna be fine on your own; they know already."

Alex was in her car and driving away before I could ask what she meant. When I looked at Maddox, his arms were folded, his usual shit-eating grin on his face.

"She texted us while you were talking to Lucia," he explained.

"She did?" I shook my head. "I'm sorry—"

"Stop." Maddox held up his hand, then put his arm around my shoulders. "First of all, she threatened that anyone who gave you shit would answer to her. Second…" Maddox turned so he was facing me. "Ainsley, did you really think we'd be upset about this?"

That Maddox was being uncharacteristically serious almost broke my heart. Now that it was out in the open, I realized I should've given in and told them long ago.

While I'd feared they'd be mad, I was wrong. Maddox was hurt.

"I don't know…"

"How could I be mad, Ains? Alex and I were doing the same thing."

"I'm sorry, Maddox. I just…I don't know."

"Okay, you're sorry. It's over. Let's move on." He walked toward the porch, but stopped halfway. "At least you picked the one I actually like."

"What about Gabe? You like him, don't you? And Enzo? And—"

"Kidding, Ains. Although—being serious for a minute—as far as you're concerned, Cris is the only one who comes close to measuring up."

I looked out at the vineyards. "I've loved him practically my whole life."

Maddox winked. "I know the feeling, sweetheart."

5

Ainsley

Naughton's reaction to finding out Cris and I were together wasn't any different than Maddox's, although he didn't say as much. That didn't worry me, though. Naughton had always been the quiet one in our family.

"What's happening tonight?" I asked. Both Naughton and Cris shrugged.

"Don't know what the women are doing," Naughton said, "but we're planning a guys' night out."

"Wait," said Maddox. "We can't go out tonight."

"Why not?" asked Naught. "Oh. Never mind. Damn, Mad, Brodie's gonna be a father. How long does it take anyway?"

"It can vary quite a bit." Cris spoke for the first time since Alex and I arrived.

I walked over and wove my hand with his. "How's it going?" I whispered.

"Everything's fine," he whispered back, but not quietly.

Maddox wrapped his arm around my neck and led me away from Cris. "You're outta your league, sister, when it comes to keepin' secrets. Ain't nobody ever gonna break my record."

"Thanks, Mad."

"Oh, by the way, Alex asked me to give you this." My brother handed something to Cris.

"What is that?" I asked.

"Keys to her beach house," Cris answered. "Told you it would work itself out."

"You're acting like we're done here, but you've forgotten one very important detail."

Cris looked at me and shrugged. "You've got me. I have no idea."

Naughton refilled Cris' wineglass, poured another, and handed it to me. "Laird and Sorcha."

"Right." Cris all but groaned. "Guess we'd better talk to them. You ready, sweetheart?"

"I was way more worried about them," I said, nodding at my brothers.

Maddox took a drink of wine and lit his cigar. "Gotta warn ya, Cris. Sorcha's gonna see this as the opportunity for more grandkids."

"Don't worry, we don't have to—"

Cris silenced me with another kiss, although this one wasn't quite as steamy as the one Alex had witnessed. When he rested his palm on my abdomen, Maddox put his hand on Cris' shoulder.

"Is she…"

"Not yet." Cris winked.

"Um…I'm right here." I slugged Maddox. "If you want to know something, ask me."

My brother rubbed his arm. "Have you been taking boxing lessons from Alex? Damn, Ains, that hurt."

"Come here," said Naughton, putting his arm around my shoulders and leading me away from Cris and Maddox. "I've been worried about you, Ains. Is this what's been eatin' at you? This thing with Cris?"

I nodded. "We broke up because I didn't want to tell anyone about us. That's what you picked up on at Brodie's wedding."

"Now you're back on?"

"Yeah. I can't believe I made such a big thing of not telling you guys."

"Bradley and I promised not to have secrets."

"It's a good plan, Naught."

I watched Cris and Maddox walk over to the two smaller houses my father had built on the property.

They went inside the one Mad had lived in before he and Alex got engaged and moved to a vineyard estate of their own.

"What were you two doing?" I asked when they came back out.

"You just never mind," Maddox answered.

Cris put his arm around my waist. "Ready?" He motioned toward the house.

We were about to go inside when my mother came barreling out the front door and down the porch steps. She stomped over to Maddox. "Why didn't you tell me Peyton is having the baby?"

"I was just on my way to, Ma," said Maddox, backing away before she could smack him.

"Tá tú liar!" She shook her head, scowled, and froze when she saw my hand in Cris'. *"Tá áthas an domhain orm!"* She kissed Cris' cheek and then pulled me away from him.

"What did she say?" I heard Cris ask Maddox.

"Ma approves. In a big way." Maddox grinned. "I'm tellin' ya; she's gonna start pestering the both of you about grandbabies."

"I'm on board," Cris said, winking at me. "How about you, Ains?"

I might've attempted a witty comeback, but the look on Cris' face was so serious. I turned back to my mother. "Where's Da?"

"Getting the car so we can go to the hospital." She walked to the side of the house and peered around the corner. "The baby will be in high school by the time he gets here. Whose is that?" She was pointing at Cris' Tesla.

"Mine," he answered.

"Good." My mother grabbed his arm. "It looks fast. Take me to the hospital." She shook her finger at me. "You ride with your da."

Five minutes later, I was in Mad's truck, along with Naughton and our father, who—Maddox decided—probably shouldn't drive.

We'd been at the hospital a little over four hours when Alex came through the double doors and into the obstetrics waiting room.

"Look!" she cried, holding up her phone. "Isn't she beautiful?"

Everyone gathered around Alex's screen, but Cris and I hung back. I pulled him around the corner, reached up, and kissed him.

"Mmm, I like this," he murmured, kissing me deeper.

"Thank you for insisting we stop hiding," I whispered.

"It's so much better together, Ains. Isn't it?"

"Where did Cris and Ainsley go?" we heard Alex ask. "I'm waiting."

When we came around the corner, she had her hands on her hips. "Finally, the lovebirds show up. I'm not sure which is the bigger news. Is it Brodie and Peyton's baby or my brother, head-over-heels in love with Ainsley? I think it's gotta be a tie."

Alex held up her phone again. "This baby, who is the most beautiful child on the face of the earth, by the way, weighs seven pounds, two ounces, and her name is…I just love this name so much."

"Alex! Just tell us," I demanded.

"Kismet Kadence Butler."

It would be two years in February since we received word that our oldest brother, Kade, had been killed in the line of duty. That Brodie and Peyton honored him with the baby's middle name brought me to tears.

6

Cristobal

Was it all the talk of weddings and having babies intensifying the impatience I felt for Ainsley and me to start our own family? Or was it the relief I felt that we could finally be a normal couple around our siblings and parents?

Speaking of parents, while Sorcha knew we were together and I was sure she had already told Laird, I wanted to have my own conversation with Ainsley's dad.

When I saw him walk out into the waiting area, I approached him before anyone else could.

"I was wondering if you and I could schedule a time to talk, sir."

His eyes scrunched in a way that made his smile lines deepen. "Cristobal, I have known you since you were a wee bairn. Please call me Laird."

"Yes, sir…err…Laird. Um, I'm sure by now you've heard your daughter and I are together."

He raised a brow, but the twinkle in his eye remained. "*Living* together is what I heard."

"Yes."

He put his hand on my shoulder. "When you and Ainsley become parents, you will look back on this and realize your offspring's secrets aren't as easily kept as they believe they are."

I smiled. "How long have you known?"

"Since shortly after her twenty-first birthday."

So, the entire time. "Did Sorcha know as well?"

Laird laughed. "How do you think I found out?"

"There's something else I'd like to discuss with you, if there's time."

"I'd hoped you'd say that. Come, let's take a walk."

7

Ainsley

Even though the wedding hadn't started yet and I'd never admit it to anyone, of the three that had recently taken place, Maddox and Alex's was my favorite, and it had nothing to do with the fact that the bridesmaids' dresses the bride had picked were by far the most flattering.

The ceremony was being held in the courtyard at Demetria—Maddox and Alex's estate.

Cris, his brothers, and Naughton had helped Bradley and me decorate the space. Alex had left it to Peyton to make all the decisions about how the courtyard should look, and Peyton had made sure she had everything ready just in case she went into labor, and it was a good thing she had.

There were hundreds of twinkle lights to hang on the wrought-iron fencing and in the trees. Pots and pots of amaryllis, paperwhites, and poinsettias were scattered around the yard and in the winery, where the reception would be held.

I was upstairs in the villa, which was adjacent to Demetria's vineyards, getting ready with Bradley, Peyton, and Alex, waiting impatiently for the latter to relinquish her hold on baby Kismet.

"My turn," I said, taking her from Alex's arms. "You need to get dressed."

Alex pouted. "But once I do, Peyton told me I can't hold her again until after the wedding."

"She'll spit up on your dress, Alex. As soon as you and Maddox are officially married and all the photos have been taken, you can hold her again," said the baby's mother.

"I can't wait." Alex rubbed her tummy.

I caught a look that passed between Alex, Peyton, and Bradley. "You're not talking about holding Kismet later, are you?"

Alex shook her head and smiled.

"Oh my God," I shouted, racing over to hug my soon-to-be sister-in-law with one arm while I held the baby with the other.

"You, too?" I asked Bradley, who smiled.

"Not yet, but we're definitely working on it."

"How do you look this good already?" Alex asked Peyton. "You had a baby five minutes ago, and you already look like you did before you got pregnant."

"It's been a couple of days, Alex. Plus, this dress is very forgiving." Peyton smoothed the folds of the sleeveless dress Alex had chosen for us to wear. The design and color of Peyton's were a little different than the ones Bradley and I wore. Instead of emerald green, Peyton's was a shimmery gold, and instead of being fitted, the one she wore had a high waist.

"A couple days." Alex rolled her eyes.

"You really went from the pan to the fire, or the fire to the pan, whatever that expression is," I said to Bradley. "You get married, then are in two more weddings in two months. Are you overwhelmed yet?"

Before she could answer, Alex put her arm around Bradley's shoulders. "She's part of the family."

My cheeks flushed. "I didn't mean anything by that."

"I know what you meant," said Bradley. "And so did Alex. I don't have any sisters, and my mom died when I was twelve. I've always been close to my aunt, but I've never had…" Bradley started to cry.

"Uh-oh," said Alex and Peyton at the same time.

"What?" I asked.

"Cue the pregnancy test." Alex laughed and stepped behind the screen to change.

Bradley's eyes opened wide, but then she shrugged. "Like I said, we've been trying."

"Are you ready? I expect gasps, hand-clapping, and even catcalls if you're so inclined," Alex said from behind a screened partition.

When she came into view, no one made a single sound. I didn't know about Peyton or Bradley, but I was too stunned to speak. I'd never seen a gown like the one Alex wore, or a more beautiful bride.

"Speechless? Is that how you're going to play this?"

"You're stunning," Bradley finally whispered.

The dress was made of antique lace that looked as though Alex wasn't wearing anything beneath it. It had long sleeves, a drop waist, and at the front, two slits opened partway down Alex's thighs.

When she turned around, I saw the gown dipped low in the back and had the same slits as the front. Only a woman of Alex's height and slight frame would be able to wear a dress like this off. As short as I was, I would look ridiculous in it.

"You're going to bring Maddox to his knees," said Peyton, smiling. "I have no doubt that's what you're going for."

The door opened, and Alex ducked behind the screen. She came out when she saw it was her mother and mine walking in.

Both had the same reaction. They gasped first, cried, then said things in their own native languages that no one else in the room understood. It wasn't necessary, though. The looks on each of the women's faces mirrored Peyton's, Bradley's, and mine from moments ago.

"Is it time?" Alex asked.

"Si, mija," Lucia answered, dabbing her tears.

"May I have a moment?" my mom asked, looking around the room and waiting until everyone left, including me, who closed the door. I was tempted to leave it open just a crack to hear what she was saying to Alex, but I didn't.

A minute later, the door opened and Alex stepped out, following my mother, who led the way down the staircase.

It wasn't until we were all standing at the bottom of the steps that Alex turned around to show us the gift my mom had given her.

Wearing a *luckenbooth* brooch was a Scottish wedding tradition, and I recognized the one Alex wore. It was made of gold, and the crown that sat above two intertwined hearts was encrusted with diamonds and rubies. I remembered my mom saying it had been given to her by my grandmother on my father's side.

The tradition was that it be given to the bride of the family's oldest son right before she walked down the aisle. I didn't know whether my mother had told Alex its significance, or if Peyton, Bradley, or Lucia knew, but I did, and it brought me to tears.

When the bridesmaids stepped outside, I saw Cris standing with Brodie, Maddox, and Naughton, who was the best man.

It hadn't dawned on me until now that Cris was the only one of Alex's brothers Maddox had asked to stand with him. I hadn't realized the two were that close.

My darling Cristobal looked so handsome in his charcoal-gray tuxedo that I couldn't wait for him to take off later. His gaze traversed up and down my body, letting me know he was thinking the same thing I was.

Peyton took her place as matron of honor after Bradley and I joined the men near where the minister waited, the music being piped out onto the courtyard from the winery changed, and the door of the villa opened.

It wasn't that I hadn't seen my brother Maddox's various expressions—he had the most expressive face of all my siblings, maybe of anyone I'd ever known—but the look I saw on his face when Alex came out the door on her mother's arm was one I'd never seen before.

Everyone deserved love, and a great love at that, but what he and Alex had between them was a grand passion. The tragedy it could have been, if they hadn't finally admitted their devotion to each other, would've been Shakespearean. It was as though the two of them were made for one another, in temperament, humor, zest for life, and outright beauty.

The ceremony was traditional Presbyterian until it came to the vows, which the minister said Alex and Maddox had written to one another. They were sanctified by God, he said, but they would remain private. I was disappointed, but only because I was curious. At the same time, I was envious of a love so deep it only mattered what the other thought, no one else.

"May I have this dance, *niña bonita*."

I put my hand in Cris' and let him guide me around the makeshift dance floor set up in the tasting room.

"It was a beautiful wedding, don't you agree?" I asked, resting my cheek against his shoulder.

"Beautiful bridesmaid too."

"Your sister is glowing." I wondered if he knew Alex was pregnant, or if anyone did. Several people here tonight probably suspected it, since neither she nor Maddox had anything more than sparkling water to drink.

"Tomorrow is Christmas," Cris murmured. "Our first together."

In the past, we'd talked about telling our families we couldn't leave Palo Alto for one reason or another, just so we could spend one Christmas morning together, but neither of us had been able to go through with it.

"I guess we should decide what we're going to do tomorrow…"

Cris smiled. "We're going to sleep as late as we want to, take a walk on the beach, have breakfast—just the two of us—then, in the afternoon, we'll visit both of our families."

"Cris…I…uh…um…"

"Didn't get me anything for Christmas?"

I hadn't, but how did he always know what I was thinking?

We'd been broken up. Then after he came to the Kensey building last weekend, we'd only been apart when he was working or I was teaching, or finishing up my paperwork for the semester. I'd tried a couple of times to get something for him online, but nothing seemed right.

"I hope you didn't get anything for me…"

"Just something little, Ains." He leaned forward and brushed my lips with his. "You gave me the thing I wanted most already. The only thing I wanted."

"I'm sorry I held out for so long."

"Don't be. What did I overhear Maddox say a couple of days ago? It's over. Let's move on."

When the song we were dancing to ended, Cris led me over to where Alex and Maddox stood, talking with Peyton and Brodie, who held Kismet in his arms.

"She's so beautiful, Brodie." I kissed the baby's head.

"I'd let you hold her, but you have two people in line ahead of you."

I looked over and saw Peyton's two sons from another marriage, Jamison and Finn, waiting patiently.

"Who won the toss to go next?" I asked.

Finn raised his hand in the air. "I did!"

"Because you cheated," said Jamison.

"Did not."

The older of the two shook his head. "It doesn't matter. Even if I got to hold her first, you'd just be bugging me every five seconds for your turn anyway."

"I doubt any of you ever argued over holding me." I nudged Brodie, who shook his head, and then sat next to Finn, making sure he cradled his sister's head and held her tight, but not too tight.

I leaned back, thinking it was Cris standing behind me, but Maddox rested his hands on my shoulders. I peeked at the ring on his left hand, then turned around and noticed Cris dancing with Alex.

"I like your ring."

"Scottish thistle."

I rolled my eyes. "Yes, Mad. I know."

"Have you seen Al's ring?"

I had, but until Alex pulled me aside to show it off, I hadn't realized that the first time she saw it, was when my brother slipped it on her finger during the ceremony.

"I can't believe you chose the same thing for each other, with neither of you knowing it."

Alex's ring had a Scottish thistle design as well, but far more elaborate than Mad's. Hers was made of platinum, with one large diamond in the center and several smaller ones all around the band.

"You know why we never fought over holding you?" he asked.

"I was just joking, Maddox."

"I'm not. It's because Kade was always first. He'd spend hours sitting on the front porch, rocking you to sleep. Even after you'd closed your eyes, he'd still hold you. Ma would scold him, saying you'd never go to sleep on your own if he held you so much, but he ignored her."

"He ignored Ma? You had me convinced until you added that, Maddox. Tell me the truth, did Kade even hold me once?"

"It's true, lass," said our mother, who I hadn't realized was listening.

Right after Maddox asked our mother to dance, Naughton joined me, tweaking my cheek. "You look about a million times better than you did at the last wedding."

"Thanks, Naught. I appreciate the compliment so much."

"I heard you and Mad talking about Kade. I remember him holding you all the time."

"I bet you weren't second in line."

I caught the flash of hurt on his face. "I'm sorry. That wasn't funny."

"I guess you owed me one since I just told you, you looked like shit at Brodie's wedding."

I slugged him. "You're hysterical, Naughton."

I watched Brodie help Finn hand the baby to his brother. "It's sad, though, isn't it?"

"What's that, Ains?"

"That Kade isn't here to see Maddox get married, just like he wasn't at your wedding or Brodie's."

Naughton put his arm around me and kissed my forehead. "We all miss him, sweetheart."

8

Ainsley

When we parked in the driveway of Alex's beach house, the first thing I noticed was a tree, decorated and lit, in the front window.

"Isn't that sweet? With everything going on, she still got a Christmas tree. Wow."

Cris smiled and nodded, but once we were inside, I realized my mistake. Alex hadn't gotten a tree; Cris had, and somehow, he'd managed to sneak a box of decorations here with him.

We'd always decorated a tree and celebrated an early Christmas, just the two of us, before we went home to our families.

"As beautiful as you look in this dress, I need you naked, Ains."

I smiled and tugged at his lapels. "I've been waiting for the same thing since I first saw you standing with my brothers in this tuxedo."

We stripped out of our wedding clothes and sat naked, wrapped in a blanket by the tree. It didn't feel much different than those other Christmases, except this year, we wouldn't go our separate ways tomorrow.

For the first time in six years, we'd celebrate the holiday together. My only regret tonight was that I didn't have any gifts for him to open in the morning.

"I love you, Ainsley," Cris said as though—once again—he'd read my thoughts.

"Cris, I…"

"Love me, too? Is that what you were about to say?" He leaned forward and kissed me. "That's all I want for Christmas, *mi amor*." He kissed me again and eased me onto my back. "Actually, I did think of something else I want. I've missed your freckles."

I giggled. "Since this morning?"

He ran his tongue from my neck down to my breasts. "These are my favorite." He traced a line over my skin with his fingertips, ending at my right nipple. "Although I really like these too."

I arched my back when he sucked the tip into his mouth and squeezed my flesh with one hand while the other cupped my pussy.

"I need to be inside you, Ains. Nothing between us."

We'd never made love without a condom, and that had been at my request. "I want that too, Cris."

I shuddered when he eased his hardness inside me.

"Oh my God," he groaned, stilling for a minute before taking me hard like he knew I wanted. "I love you, Ainsley."

Cris and I had made love hundreds of times, yet tonight felt different, new almost. It was more than that there was no barrier between us. Now that we'd been honest with our families, it felt like our love had deepened.

It was close to five in the morning when something startled me awake. I thought I'd heard a noise, but Cris hadn't budged, so maybe I'd been dreaming.

I stretched, slid out of bed, and found one of Alex's robes hanging on the back of the bedroom door. I padded to the bathroom, but noticed the Christmas tree lights were still on. I could've sworn Cris had turned them off before we'd gone to bed, but maybe they were on a timer.

Instead of going back to sleep, I crept into Alex's kitchen to make coffee.

In the third cupboard I opened, I found coffee beans as well as a French press and a copper kettle to heat water in. I studied the kettle while I filled it; something about it looked familiar. Maybe my parents had one like it. I turned around to put it on the stove, and almost screamed when I saw someone standing outside the back door.

"Da? What are you doing here?" I whispered when he put his finger to his lips, shushing me. "Come in."

"Just for a minute." He brushed past me and set a box on the counter. "I was supposed to give this to you last night, and I forgot. Your ma saw it this morning and insisted I drive it over here."

My mother had always gotten up long before dawn—probably the result of being married to a vineyard owner for so many years.

"What is it?"

"I don't know, Ainsley. It's for you, but it's heavy."

He stepped forward and kissed my cheek. "Merry Christmas, my beloved child."

"Merry Christmas, Da. Please, tell Ma we'll be over later."

When the kettle started to hum, I raced over to turn the heat off before it woke Cris. When I turned back around, my father was gone.

I peeked inside the box and saw a wrapped present. I tried to lift the gift out, but it was too heavy, so I tilted the outer box instead and slid it onto the counter.

The tag read, "Cristobal," in handwriting similar to my own. Since my mother's and mine were almost identical, I assumed it was a gift for him from my parents. At least he'd have one gift to open this morning, even if it wasn't from me.

"What's this? Did I miss Santa?" Cris walked into the kitchen, bare-chested, hair disheveled, his pajama bottoms hanging loosely on his hips. He was, without question, the sexiest man on the planet.

All my life, I'd loved Cristobal Avila, from the first time I'd laid eyes on him. I'd been a little girl then, but somehow, I knew that one day, he'd love me, too. It's why I'd only applied to Stanford and why I never gave up on him, even when he'd acted as though he wasn't even interested in being my friend.

We'd talked about it many times, and I still found it hard to believe that he'd secretly wanted me too, as he'd said, from the day he first saw me sitting in the quad. It was only the idea that I was too young for him that kept him from acting on my "magnetic pull," as he'd called it.

"I felt the same pull from you," I'd told him then. "It's the same way I described it."

To think I'd almost lost him.

Cris cupped my cheek with his palm. "What is it, *niña bonita*?"

I shook my head. "It's nothing."

"Tell me," he coaxed.

"I'm just really happy we're together."

"Merry Christmas." He wrapped his arms around me and cupped my bottom, drawing me closer to him. "Why are we up so early?" he murmured.

"My father…" I nuzzled into him, and Cris stepped back.

"Your father?"

I laughed at the stunned look on his face. "He was here. But now he's gone."

"He was here?"

"He forgot to give me that last night." I motioned toward the box on the counter. "It's for you." I pointed at the wrapped gift. "I'm sorry to confess it isn't from me."

"Who is it from?"

"My parents, I think, but it's odd that they wouldn't just give it to you later. They know we're coming over."

"Hold that thought. I'll be right back." Cris walked back down the hallway, I assumed to use the bathroom. I finished making coffee.

When he returned, I was disappointed to see he'd put on a Stanford hoodie and his hands were in the front pocket.

"Are you cold? We could light a fire."

"That's an excellent idea." Cris stacked two logs in Alex's fireplace, tossed some newspaper in, and lit it. "Do I smell coffee?"

"It'll be ready in a few minutes. I was thinking about making breakfast, but I don't know if Alex has much…"

I opened the refrigerator door and found orange juice, eggs, fresh vegetables, and bacon. I smiled. "You?"

Cris nodded and smiled too.

Side by side, we made omelets and bacon, just like we usually did on the weekend. Cris took out a loaf of fresh sourdough bread and made toast.

"Should we eat at the counter?" Cris asked, not waiting for me to answer before picking up the package that sat on it. "Whoa. This is heavy." He set it at the base of the tree. "What's in it?"

I shrugged. "I honestly have no idea."

"I can't imagine a better Christmas morning," Cris said between bites of his breakfast.

"Me either, and I like this place." I'd felt comfortable the minute we stepped inside last night, and while I'd never been here before, I felt like I had. If Cris hadn't just started Geneco and I weren't at Stanford, finishing my PhD, I could see us living in a place on the beach just like this. Compared to what we could get in Palo Alto for the average cost of houses in the area, Alex's twelve-hundred-square-foot house was practically a mansion.

Cris took my plate and his to the sink. "Presents now, or back to bed and presents later?"

"Oh, back to bed. Definitely."

The sun had been up for at least two hours when we sat by the Christmas tree again.

"What's that?" I asked, noticing a small package sitting on top of the one for Cris.

"I don't know. Let's go see." Cris led me over to an armchair. "Looks like our fire's out. I'll get it going again."

"You were busy," I said while he stoked the wood. "The tree, the groceries, the gifts…"

Cris knelt in front of me. "I wanted it to be perfect, Ainsley." He held out the package that had been sitting on top of his gift. "Open it."

"Aren't you going to open yours?"

"In a minute."

I untied the ribbon and gasped when I tore the paper and saw it was a ring box. Cris took it from my hand then and looked into my eyes.

"Ainsley, my sweet Ainsley. Will you marry me?" He'd opened the lid, but I couldn't see its contents through my tears.

"Yes, I'll marry you," I cried. Before I could say anything else, Cris kissed me.

"I love you, Ainsley." He took my left hand in his and slid the ring on my finger. It was a perfect fit.

"I love you, too, Cris."

"Do you like it?"

"I love it."

"You haven't even looked at it," he teased.

"I still love it." I rested my hand on his and gasped a second time when I looked more closely at the ring he'd given me.

It was similar to Alex's Scottish thistle ring, but at the same time, very different. "Gold is better with your skin," he murmured as I studied the setting and the stones adorning it. There were small emeralds in the shape of a heart and, in its center, a princess-cut diamond. I'd seen so many traditional Scottish rings in my lifetime, but none as beautiful as this one.

Cris wiped the tears from my cheek. "Happy?"

"So far beyond happy."

He smiled and looked over at the fire.

"Open yours now. I'm sorry it—"

"Shh. I told you, Ainsley. I've gotten everything I wanted for Christmas. There could be no better gift."

I rested my head on his shoulder and wrapped my arms around him. "Open it anyway," I whispered.

Cris sat on the floor and brought the package closer to him. "It feels like books." He raised an eyebrow. "Are you suggesting it's time I go back to school?"

I held up my hands. "Not from me. Remember?"

He tore the paper from the box and lifted its lid.

I peeked over his shoulder and gasped at the same time he did.

"Ainsley…I'm speechless."

So was I. The books in the box were familiar to me. They had been among my brother Kade's most prized possessions. I remembered when he'd found them in the back of an old bookstore—although, now, I couldn't recall where it had been, only his excitement at finding them.

The set, in original and rare morocco binding, was a first-edition collection of the works of Charles Darwin. It was priceless, but more so to Cris because of the work he did.

The bindings showed wear and had dark spots here and there, but inside, the engraved illustrations were in perfect condition.

"I…I…" Cris laughed. "I'm literally speechless. Ainsley…I…They're incredible…It's incredible."

My head was reeling. Kade had *known*. Somehow, he'd found out I was in love with Cristobal and that he would treasure, and know the value of, this collection far more than most anyone else would.

It wasn't about the monetary value of the books, though. The real gift was what they meant, particularly to a man of science.

I watched Cris as he gently touched each volume, opened it, and marveled at its contents, shaking his head again and again.

He set the book he held on the blanket by the tree, reached into the box, and took out an envelope.

"This is for you."

I recognized the handwriting—it was my brother's. I realized then it was the same as what was on Cris' gift.

My dear baby sister—

I wonder if you know how precious you were to me. Ma always said it was up to me to tell you that, when you were born, I was the one who chose your name.

It means meadow, but to me, it means every delicate flower, every fragile leaf, every blade of grass that blows gently in the breeze.

Your heart is full of everything beautiful found in the meadows around Butler Ranch, where I was so blessed to watch you grow up.

You may know by now that I was aware of your feelings for Cristobal. He is a fine and good man, who will love you even more than you love him. In my heart, I know you are meant to be together, just as you've always known.

All my love,
Kade

I wasn't sure how long Cris held me as I cried. He ran his fingers through my hair, caressed me, loved me, and took care of me, just like Kade knew he would.

"Your brother loved you so much, Ains."

"I can't believe he knew about us."

"Not just him." Cris told me about the conversation he'd had with my father yesterday.

"You're saying they all knew? Just like we knew about Maddox and Alex?"

"Not everyone. No offense, sweetheart, but I don't think your brothers have the same IQ as you and your parents do. Or maybe it's a lack of social awareness."

I shrugged. There'd been a time I might've thought they didn't know because they didn't care. The conversations I'd had with them over the last two days, coupled with Kade's letter, proved me wrong.

9

Cristobal

The sound of Ainsley's laughter carried across the room, warming my heart. It wasn't as though I hadn't seen her around her family. We'd both been at winery events over the years, but none where I could walk over, move her hair away from her neck, and kiss the soft skin beneath her ear.

"I know that look," said Maddox, handing me a glass of wine. "And, yeah, it's weird you're looking at my sister that way, but I guess it's just as weird for you when you catch me lusting after Alex."

I shook my head and laughed. "You're right. Not something I want a mental image of."

"Tough shit. You fell in love with her; you're stuck with us too."

"I love her so much," I said, almost under my breath.

"Pretty damn obvious, dude."

"I asked her to marry me."

"Yeah? Lemme guess. New Year's Eve?"

I chuckled. "I'd be happy to do it tomorrow. Something tells me your sister will want more time than that to plan."

"That's what I thought about your sister." He took a drink of wine. "Sure proved me wrong."

"Alex is pregnant, isn't she?"

Maddox let out a heavy sigh and smiled. "Yeah."

"Congratulations."

"Gotta admit, I'm holding my breath, praying it goes okay."

"It will. I'll talk with her before we head home. There are a few things I can prescribe, none of which are actual prescriptions."

"You're a good man, Cris."

I looked over at him, but he was looking at his sister.

"You take damn good care of her, you hear me?"

"Loud and clear."

Ainsley was sitting cross-legged on the floor, but stood and walked over to me at the same time her brother walked away.

"You're older than him. You don't have to take his shit," she teased.

I pulled her into my arms. "That may be true, but his arms alone are twice my size." Her back was to my front, and she leaned into me.

"How long do you want to stay?" she asked.

"Here at the house or in town?"

"Both."

"In either case, I'm in no hurry. What about you?"

"I know it sounds weird, but something tells me we shouldn't go back to Palo Alto right away."

A week later, we knew why.

10

Ainsley

"Did you know Alex and Maddox were on their way over?" I asked Cris, who was sitting on the floor in the living room, looking at the books I—or Kade—had given him for Christmas.

"I didn't." He stood, walked over to me, and looked out the kitchen window at his sister and my brother.

"Something's up." Neither looked sad, but they didn't look happy either.

I raced to the door, only realizing once I'd opened it that I was, in essence, about to invite Alex into her own house.

"Hey, Ains," said Maddox, wrapping me in a hug. I looked at Alex, whose eyes filled with tears. She took a step back.

"What's wrong?" Cris came over and put his arm around my waist.

"Have a seat, sweetheart," said my brother.

My eyes filled with tears like Alex's had. "No. Tell me and get it over with."

"This is good news, Ainsley," said Alex, reaching for my hand, but I jerked it away.

"Just *fucking* tell me."

Maddox looked from me to Cris. "Don't let go," he muttered.

"Dammit, Maddox—"

"Ainsley, Kade is alive."

"What?" I gasped at the same time everything around me faded to black.

"I told you to sit down," I heard Maddox say when I opened my eyes. I was in Cris' arms, and we were on the sofa.

"Did you really say—" My eyes filled with tears, and I couldn't speak.

Alex sat beside us and held my hand. "It's true, Ainsley. He's really alive."

"Where?"

"He's with Brodie and Peyton right now, but your parents are hosting a dinner tonight."

My mind was reeling. "How?"

"We don't know all the details yet, but he's home, and he's healthy, and that's all that matters," said my brother.

"Right. That's all that matters."

I looked into Cris' smiling eyes. "My big brother is *alive*."

He leaned down and kissed me. "I heard."

Two hours later, I raced into my parents' house and into Kade's arms.

"You have some explaining to do," I whispered when he picked me up and twirled me in a circle while I cried tears of joy. "I heard that when I was a baby, you held me all the time."

"Sure did."

"Maddox said you wouldn't let me go, even when Ma threatened you."

He stroked my cheek and brushed away a tear. "That sounds right."

"Now, it's my turn. I'm never letting you go."

"Deal."

Even when he set me on my feet, I couldn't take my eyes off him.

"Come on, there's someone I want you to meet."

We walked over to Cris, who was talking to a woman I didn't recognize.

"Merrigan Shaw, meet my youngest sister, Ainsley." Kade leaned in close to me and whispered,

"I haven't told anyone else this, but someday, I'm going to marry her."

"I guess you already knew I was going to marry him," I said when Cris put his arm around my shoulders.

Kade shrugged and winked. "How do you like the books?"

"I was just hoping you wouldn't ask for them back."

My brother laughed. "When I found them, I knew they'd be yours someday."

Right Before Christmas

***

One Year Later

11

Laird

I walked down the steps, past the drive, to the edge of the vineyards, and turned back to look at the house where Sorcha and I had raised all six of our children. Even I'd been raised in it. So many wonderful memories were made in the home my father, Broderick Butler, had built.

He'd emigrated from Scotland in his early twenties and settled on the Central Coast of California, where he found work as one of several hundred craftsmen hired to construct Hearst Castle. There, Broderick met my mum, Analise, a seamstress who also hailed from Scotland.

The two scrimped and saved until they had enough money set aside to purchase the ranch land that was passed down to me, their only son.

The residence was built in the style of a historic Scottish Highland farmhouse with a dressed granite facade under a slate roof. It had four front dormers that were embellished with black shutters like those on the windows of the main level.

After my parents passed away, I added a porch which wrapped around all three sides of the U-shaped abode so, regardless of the season, Sorcha and I could admire the courtyard it surrounded. I'd put in a small pond and an archway that led to a path to the original barn, which my boys and I'd converted into part of the winery.

I'd also built two Scottish-style stone cottages, both two-storied replications of the main house—one in which Sorcha and I lived now.

"Would you like to ride to the hospital together?" my third oldest son, Naughton, hollered from the front porch.

"Aye, Naught."

"I'll let Bradley know we're leaving."

Naughton went back inside. The main house was his now and had been since right after he and his wife, Bradley, were married. Three months ago, they gave Sorcha and me our eighth grandchild. A boy named Charlie.

Number nine arrived a week ago. Our oldest son, Kade, and his wife, Merrigan, had named the boy for me—Laird.

"Ready, Da?" Naughton pulled his car up to where I stood.

I got in the front seat and loosened the scarf I'd worn when I came outside this morning. At first I'd walked right past it, but then Sorcha's daily reminder echoed in my head.

"'Tis colder than you think out there. Don't catch a chill, husband." Some days, she warned me that if I did, it might turn into pneumonia. How ironic that was what she herself suffered from now.

"Maddox called. He spent the night, and Brodie just got there."

"Aye," I said, nodding. It was good she wasn't alone. Sorcha never liked to be, and in the forty-six years we were together, I'd made certain it rarely happened. It was only her insistence I return to the ranch last night that made me leave. When he saw my reluctance, our second-oldest son offered to stay. Sorcha had scoffed, but didn't push him to leave.

"Kade is planning to visit today as well."

I shook my head. "He shouldn't." With a brand-new baby at home, my eldest should not risk the bairn getting ill through his papa.

Naughton chuckled. "You try to stop him."

"Aye," I said again. "There's no doubt he's his mother's son."

When Naught drove up to the main entrance of the hospital and the valet opened my door, Maddox walked out the hospital doors. His face was ashen.

"What's happened?"

"Let's get inside."

I allowed him to put his arm through mine.

"Ma is in intensive care. Her oxygen levels plummeted suddenly."

I studied him without speaking.

"Can we see her?" Naught asked, coming in behind us.

"Da can in an hour, they're saying."

Once in the elevator, I closed my eyes and leaned against the back wall. My Sorcha had faced far worse than pneumonia and beaten it.

The odds were against her survival the day I first held the woman with the fiery-red hair in my arms, certain that was where she'd die. However, when she opened her deep blue eyes and stared into mine, I raced—carrying her battered body—to the nearest medic and begged him to save her life.

It was a story none of our children had ever heard, except Kade and even he didn't know the full extent of it.

The day would come for my two daughters to hear it, but today, I'd be telling Maddox, Naughton, and Brodie. It was time they knew the true nature of the life their mother and I lived.

I led them into one of the private rooms reserved for those with family members in the ICU. "Have a seat, boys," I said, closing the door behind us. "I've a story to tell you."

Belfast, Northern Ireland, June 1972

My undercover assignment was for the CIA and MI6 jointly, serving on the security team for the UK's Secretary of State for Northern Ireland. My real objective, though, was to infiltrate the Provisional Irish Republican Army in such a way that would allow me to get close to the organization's leaders.

I preceded the secretary into the building where a secret meeting between him and representatives from PIRA would be taking place. As we were to be the first to arrive, I drew my sidearm when I entered the room and there were two men already seated at the negotiation table.

"Stand down," the secretary instructed us. While I holstered my gun, I didn't take my eyes off the men who had been among my primary targets for the past twelve months.

While I'd expected the organization to be represented by high-ranking members in order to negotiate a ceasefire, I'd received no intelligence indicating it would be by PIRA's chief of staff along with the Belfast Brigade's Commanding Officer.

Their presence made one thing abundantly clear—PIRA was in far greater turmoil than British and US intelligence believed.

I listened as the secretary laid out the first-round proposal for a ceasefire.

When I heard what the republicans were requiring in order to agree to it, I knew the meeting would go nowhere. The first, and completely unrealistic, demand was a total British withdrawal from Northern Ireland within three years.

Second, and equally absurd, was that all republican prisoners were to be released regardless of the charge against them.

The British government might as well not have scheduled the meeting at all, given they themselves were offering next to nothing besides allowing a peaceful republic opposition dismantle.

While the secretary promised to bring the counter-offers back to the British government, everyone in the room—including the two men from PIRA—knew full well it was only a stopgap to temporarily end the violence and carnage that began in the spring of 1970.

The ceasefire lasted a total of thirteen days, ending with what was dubbed the Springhill massacre, during which British snipers killed five and wounded two.

Within five days, another twelve deaths occurred, some on the British side, some PIRA, and the others were civilians.

It had never been my intention to get involved in intelligence. It was technology that intrigued me. At the age of fifteen, I'd taught myself the two main programming languages at the time—FORTRAN and COBOL.

In college, I pursued dual degrees in mathematics and engineering, two subjects that turned out to be rudimentary, in my opinion. Rather than wasting time, I completed both in under two years, then spent the next two on dual graduate programs.

Looking back on it, it was understandable why the Central Intelligence Agency as well as Her Majesty's Secret Intelligence Service took an interest in my educational pursuits, along with the patents I'd been filing. I was an American-born child of two parents born in the United Kingdom. Thus giving me duality in citizenship.

I refused to work directly for either agency, a rarity at the time. However, my motivation wasn't a lack of loyalty or allegiance to either nation. Instead, I wanted to patent and own my inventions. To take it a step further, I wanted to control how the technology was used. All were lessons I'd learned following the career of a man named Oppenheimer.

It was the CIA who'd initially hired me to work in Northern Ireland. America's agenda was more about eliminating the drain the Troubles were taking on British intelligence, thus diverting their attention from the Cold War.

It was by dumb luck that I'd listened in on the warning call that came into the Public Protection Agency at thirteen hundred hours on the twenty-first day of July. It was a day that changed my life in ways I never could've imagined and nearly ended my career in intelligence at the young age of twenty-four.

"Why is that date familiar?"

"Not likely that it would be to you, Maddox, but it is known as Bloody Friday. It was the day PIRA let the Brits know what they thought of their unwillingness to negotiate. Nine people died, and over one hundred thirty were injured, some severely."

I studied my three sons, none of whom appeared surprised by my tale. I suppose it had something to do with learning their oldest brother was not only alive, but had a career different than the one they believed. One closer to what his parents once had—and to a certain extent, still did.

"The only one who mattered to me personally was your ma."

The first of the explosions—a car bomb—occurred at fourteen hundred ten hours. There were no injuries, but several buses and surrounding buildings were destroyed.

Over the course of the next eighty minutes, bombs continued to go off all over the city of Belfast, turning it into a war zone.

British troops along with intelligence operatives, like myself, were dispatched throughout the city as reports of bomb detonations came in about every five minutes.

I was positioned with the Royal Ulster Constabulary when a second call came in, warning of a bomb at Oxford Street, the busiest bus terminal in all of Northern Ireland. When an armored patrol and helicopter were sent, something in my gut told me I would be needed. I ignored direct orders, raced to the heli, and climbed in right before the door closed.

When we landed, the scene was chaos. While most of us worked to evacuate the area, two of our agents, later reported as British soldiers, searched for the bomb. It exploded before it could be defused, killing both.

I saw a woman with fiery-red hair go down right after the blast and raced over to her. There were hundreds injured, but I was drawn to her. As I gathered her in my arms, careful of her back and left arm where it appeared she'd suffered the most injury, her deep blue eyes opened and she looked up at me.

I expected her to die before I could get to the medic I saw a short distance away, but she hung on.

"That's Rua," the man said to me and then shouted at someone else, "We need to get her in the transport!"

I helped place her on the stretcher and followed her to the medivac chopper. They didn't want to let me in, but I flashed both CIA and MI6 credentials, not that they should've done any good, but it worked.

"This is Rua?" I asked the first medic. The woman was an enigma. Some said the name was given to a group of agents rather than a single person. With her injuries, it was impossible to guess her age; however, she couldn't be more than twenty-five. To my knowledge, no one had ever known what she looked like, outside of her bosses at MI6. Those days were over.

He nodded. "We can't keep her in Belfast."

"Can this thing get to Dublin?"

"Aye."

From there, I called in every favor I could to get her taken to Ramstein. It was later confirmed the woman was in fact Sorcha Seward—the infamous Rua—whose cover was blown that day.

I lost track of the number of times she was in and out of intensive care and on the brink of death due to infections from her injuries. She had scarring on her arm and back from the shrapnel and other debris that pummeled her body.

***

We heard a knock on the door, and a nurse stuck her head in. "Mr. Butler? You can see your wife now."

I met the eyes of each of my sons, and in them, I saw tears like the ones in mine.

"Thank you for telling us the story, Da," said Maddox.

"You'll get your mother to tell you the rest."

12

Sorcha

When I was sick, I had the craziest dreams. Especially when they'd go on, no matter how many times I'd wake up. I wouldn't mind as much if they were pleasant dreams like of my Laird and I walking through the vineyards or sitting on the porch of our house at the ranch. Instead, it was always work, and something I could never finish, no matter how long the bloody thing went on.

Or I'd dream that someone was chasing me. Sometimes I even dreamed about the day of the bombing in Belfast. Those were the worst. Not dreams—nightmares.

"Sorcha, *macushla. Dùisg a-nis.*" I could hear my sweet husband's voice, feel him stroking my forehead with his fingertips. If only I could do as he asked and wake up. All I needed to do was open my eyes. Why was it so hard?

"Laird?" I tried to speak, but I couldn't hear my own voice.

"Come on, Rua. Open your eyes."

O chan eil. It was the dream again. I was back in Ramstein, fighting to live, and Laird was by my side, not letting me give up.

When I felt my eyes dampen with tears of frustration, it was as though my brain engaged. I eased my lids open and saw the face of my beloved. Not the man from forty-six years ago, but the gray-haired, weathered-skinned version of my husband. Still as devilishly handsome. I tried to reach out to cup his cheek, but my hand wouldn't listen any better than my eyelids had.

"Damnadh," I muttered, wishing I could get the oxygen mask off my face. "Where am I?"

"You're in the intensive care unit."

"Remove this thing." I shook my head and wiggled my nose.

Laird shook his head too. "I cannot."

I tried again to raise my hand. Before I could get it more than an inch, my husband held it.

"Now, Sorcha, you know what you need to do. Follow the rules so I can take you home. It's only a few days until Christmas."

"Argh. Christmas. What's to be done? Who will do it all?"

"You have four sons, two daughters, two sons-in-law, and four daughters-in-law."

"Only one son-in-law. Ainsley and Cristobal aren't married."

"Soon enough."

I closed my eyes and said a silent prayer he was right. Since they were engaged last year, neither my daughter nor her fiancé had mentioned their wedding or any plans for it. Ainsley wasn't even interested in picking out a dress for herself or the bridesmaids she hadn't figured out yet.

Laird ran his finger across my brow. "Stop fretting, my love. Will do no good."

"What's to be done?" I repeated.

"Our youngest will do what makes her happy."

"Aye."

"I told our sons the story of how we met."

My eyes opened. "You *dinnae* think to ask me first?"

"It's time, Sorcha. Time for Skye and Ainsley to hear it too."

"They won't forgive us," I whispered. "All the lies."

"I'll let you see for yourself." He left the room and came back a couple of minutes later.

"Hey, Ma," said Maddox, kissing my forehead. "How are you feeling?"

My eyes scrunched. "Is that all you have to ask me?"

My second-oldest laughed. "If you mean about the badass secret agent you used to be, I figure we have hours of stories to listen to. I, for one, can't wait."

"Me either," said Brodie.

I watched Naughton. He hadn't spoken, but it wasn't like him to do so until he was sure about what he wanted to say. He looked up, perhaps feeling my gaze on him.

"It didn't come as that much of a surprise, Ma," he said. "As far as the badass agent you *used* to be, my guess is you still are, in the same way Da is."

I smiled. Of all my children, he was the most like me. So intuitive. "Many secrets."

"Yeah?" said Maddox. "Name one family member, outside of the grandkids, most of whom can't talk yet, who hasn't kept secrets."

He was right, but had they learned to do so from their father and me?

"I want to hear as many stories as you'll tell us," said Brodie. "Everyone will."

The door opened, and a nurse walked in. "What are you all doing in here? One visitor is what I said, and then only for five minutes!"

There were only three women who could order my boys or husband around. They'd learned long ago not to tempt fate when their sisters or I issued an edict. Actually, for each, there was one more—their wife. But this nurse? I laughed.

"The doctor is on his way in," she muttered, checking the machines positioned around me.

"Good that they're here to hear."

Her mouth was pursed, but I doubted she'd challenge any of us again. I was right. She didn't.

Ten minutes later, the doctor I'd seen yesterday walked in the door.

"Your oxygen levels are much better, Mrs. Butler. However, they haven't gotten to the point where I can let you go home."

"'Tis Christmas," I said.

"If you do as you're told, you'll be home for it," said Laird.

The doctor smiled. "What your husband said."

"I want this off." I pointed to the oxygen mask.

He shook his head. "The amount of oxygen you require cannot be delivered through the cannula."

When I put my hand on the mask to adjust it, Laird squeezed my shoulder. "Sorcha," he warned.

"Mind your thistle. I wasn't taking it off."

"Any other questions?" the doctor asked.

"When *can* I go home?"

"If your levels improve, tomorrow. If not—"

I held up my hand. "They'll improve."

"They won't just because you will it, Sorcha."

I leveled my gaze on my husband's handsome face. "No? Are you certain of that?"

13

Laird

The twinkle of mischief in my wife's eyes was no different than it had been forty-six years ago. Now, and then, it made me fall more in love with her every passing minute.

The day I first brought Sorcha to meet my parents, my mother and father had the same reaction. At different times, each told me they thought I'd never meet my match, but they believed I had. I agreed. Sorcha was smart, feisty, beautiful, intelligent, and adventurous.

As Naughton had said, neither she nor I were completely retired. Granted, there were no missions that took us from home. There hadn't been since our oldest was born. I traveled to consult every so often, but we'd left danger behind after Bloody Friday.

I looked up to see Sorcha and our three sons studying me. Without realizing it, I'd rested my hand on her abdomen. Our boys looked confused, but Sorcha knew exactly what I was thinking. I could tell when she put her hand on top of mine.

She'd carried six children inside her body. Nurtured them and gave them life. Every one had been an immeasurable blessing.

This year, for the first time I could remember, all of them would be with us on Christmas, along with their own children. I knew that meant everything to my wife.

"Excuse me," I said, following the doctor out of the room and into the hallway. "You said the level of oxygen my wife requires cannot be delivered via the cannula."

"That's right."

"What amount can? Ten liters?"

"Closer to five. She is on fifteen presently."

"There is one that delivers more." Up to sixty liters, in fact, although I did not say it.

The doctor shook his head. "Given your wife's age, I must recommend a methodology with proven data."

"Aye," I said, although I disagreed. I bid the man goodbye and walked over to where my next conversation wouldn't be overheard.

"Laird, how is Sorcha?" Cristobal asked, answering my call.

"She requires the HHFC cannula in order to be released."

"I see. Would you like me to take care of it?"

"Aye," I repeated. "As soon as possible." I rarely called in favors, but in this case, it was necessary.

"I'll make a call and let you know how soon Dr. Morton can be there."

"Thank you, son."

Dr. Morton was the chief physician at Stanford Medical Center as well as the man who held the patent on the HHFC.

A year ago, his son, a journalist reporting from Afghanistan, was taken hostage. Cristobal contacted me, and within hours, he was freed and on a private plane headed back to the United States.

The man would come, and he would ensure my Sorcha was home for Christmas.

When I returned to the room, my three sons were gone, but my youngest daughter had arrived—the one engaged to the man I'd just spoken to. I looked into her tear-filled eyes and then up at my wife, who held Ainsley's hand.

"Everything will work out the way it's supposed to," Sorcha said. "You and Cristobal will be married. I know it in my heart."

Ainsley's phone vibrated, and she pulled it from her pocket. "Speak of the devil." She got up and left the room. I closed the door behind her.

"What's happened?" I asked.

"Ainsley put the engagement on hold."

Interesting that Cristobal hadn't mentioned it, but then I hadn't given him the opportunity.

"Laird? *S bheil thu ag èisteachd rium*?"

"Yes, I'm listening, Sorcha."

"What are you going to do about it?"

My eyes opened wide. I should probably have asked what that meant or even expressed some kind of sympathy, but it was something I was never good at. But *do*? What was there to do?

"You need to talk to him," she said as though she'd read my mind. Which, after all these years together, was likely.

"It is not for us to get involved."

"Our daughter's heart is broken, and you don't care enough to get *involved*?"

"Now, Sorcha," I warned.

She shook her head. "You need to do something about this. *An-diugh*."

Today? I wouldn't today or any other day. I stood and leaned over, resting my hands on either side of her. "I'll not be doing anything about anything other than making sure you're home for Christmas. You are all that matters to me."

"Laird—"

I smiled and looked into her eyes. "Sorcha."

"You remember how it was, don't you? Both of us so unsure whether we were doing the right thing."

She remembered wrong. I'd never been unsure. It was she who got cold feet and wanted to postpone our wedding. I couldn't help but wonder if Cristobal was more like me, and Ainsley like her mother.

Landstuhl Medical Center, Germany, August 21, 1972

The wounds Sorcha suffered on the outside of her body had healed, leaving only scarring. Her lungs, though, still hadn't fully recovered from what was known as "blast lung."

The condition was characterized by the presence of three complications. First, apnea, or the temporary cessation of breathing. Next, bradycardia, where the heart rate dips below sixty beats per minute. As a result, the third condition was hypotension, or abnormally low blood pressure.

It was the apnea that frightened me the most as I lay awake, making sure she didn't stop breathing in her sleep.

Consequently, for most of the day and night, Sorcha had to wear what was known as a non-invasive ventilation mask. It was cumbersome for her but far better than the alternative—intubation.

Several times over the last month, her inability to take in sufficient oxygen, combined with infections caused by her other injuries, resulted in her coming close to death.

While at first the medical team at Landstuhl refused to divulge the specifics of her condition to me, that I refused to leave except to shower and change clothes, even sleeping in her room every night, made them finally accept that I was her "next of kin."

I wasn't, but Sorcha refused to allow me to contact her parents. Given that she'd often spent weeks and months undercover, not hearing from her wouldn't be out of the ordinary for her mother or father.

Her other hesitation in contacting them was that her cover had been blown; thus, they'd be in harm's way if she did. However, both the CIA and MI6 had round-the-clock protection in place for her and her parents due to the ongoing threat from PIRA.

Admittedly, I took advantage of her injuries early on, insisting we knew each other and the blast must've affected her memory.

The longer I stayed—or refused to leave—the more suspicious Sorcha became. Eventually, she asked me to tell her the details of how we'd met, and I couldn't lie.

When I reached the end of my tale, she didn't ask why a complete stranger had made sure she got out of the UK or why I had spent every day and night with her at the hospital.

"You saved my life. More than once."

"Aye." I expected her to thank me and tell me to be on my way. Instead, she reached out her hand, and I took it.

"You kissed me good night and good morning. Always on the cheek."

I nodded, my voice clogged with too much emotion to speak. I so wanted to confess that I fell in love with her the first time I held her in my arms. After calling me daft, I expected she'd call security to toss me from the room.

"Good morning here." She pointed to her left cheek. "And good night here." She pointed to her right. "Never here." Her fingertips rested on her lips. "It's time, I think, don't you?"

It took me several seconds to realize what she was suggesting. It was the twinkle in her eyes that brought me back around. "Yeah?"

"Better be quick about it before I change my mind." She winked.

When I leaned over her like I had every morning and night and brought my mouth close to hers, Sorcha put her palms on my cheeks before I could kiss her. "Thank you," she whispered.

I expected it to be as chaste as the ones I'd given her to start and end her day, but she had other ideas. Ones I was all too happy to go along with.

It was another month before she was able to leave Ramstein. Rather than returning to Scotland, the CIA made arrangements for her to be transported to the States. Unbeknownst to either of us, her parents met us in California—at the ranch owned by my parents.

I installed my first security system—one I designed, built, and put in entirely on my own—in the days right after we arrived.

While the agency assured me their detail would keep *Rua* safe, I couldn't risk losing her. In fact, I vetted each member of her team myself before they were allowed within fifty feet of her.

What I hadn't realized was *I* was the person in the most danger, from Angus Steward, Sorcha's father.

Our first night at my parents' ranch, I sneaked into the guestroom where she slept, to find him waiting for me. That he threatened to kill me if I didn't marry his daughter within a fortnight, worked in my favor, considering I'd planned to ask her anyway.

When she delayed two weeks after his deadline, it was my impending demise at her father's hands that finally made her agree to elope.

14

Sorcha

Laird was thinking about something to do with our past. He had tells. When he was lost in thought and his hand rested on my belly, he was thinking about our children.

When it rested on my shin, he was more often than not thinking about my days at Ramstein—*our* days, since he'd been with me almost every hour.

He told me once that he fell in love with me the day he carried me away from Oxford Street Station and into the waiting medical helicopter. I couldn't say I knew the exact moment it happened for me, but three months after we met, I became his wife. And I sure wouldn't have married someone I didn't love with all my heart—no matter how much my father threatened to kill Laird if we didn't hurry up and wed.

Without my da's insistence, would it have happened so quickly? Would I have put it off like my Ainsley was with Cristobal?

"You could threaten to kill him," I muttered.

Laird laughed. "I was just thinking about your father."

My husband hadn't been the one who wanted to delay. It was me. Of course, we hardly knew each other.

The same wasn't true for my daughter and her fiancé. They'd lived together for years, believing it was in secret. Maybe to everyone else, but not to me, Laird, or Cris' mother, Lucia. We'd let them think they were fooling us, believing they'd tell us in their own time.

Ainsley hesitated to reveal their relationship, but like Laird, Cristobal was forced to give her an ultimatum. That was a year ago, and on Christmas Day, he'd proposed.

I felt certain they'd be married by now, but they hadn't even begun planning the wedding. Whenever Lucia or I asked, my daughter either changed the subject or left the room.

It wasn't like me to let something like that go, but with her, something told me I needed to.

I looked up when the door opened and she came in and sat in the chair she'd occupied earlier. I felt some relief that she didn't look like she'd been crying again.

"Da, Cris wanted me to tell you that he and Dr. Morton would be here in the morning."

My ears pricked up, and I smiled. Laird must've called the man who invented the oxygen delivery device I'd tested before it was put on the market.

With it, I'd be able to go home even at my present oxygen level requirement. I'd thought to mention it when the doctor came to talk with us earlier, but forgot all about it.

I looked at my dear husband, always my savior and protector. I wished I could take away his worry about the fragility of my respiratory system. It was something we'd lived with for forty-six years and would continue to until the day I died.

Laird stroked the back of my hand with his thumb. "Your doctor may balk, but I'm confident Morton will convince him otherwise."

"If not him, his boss."

"Da, you know what I've always wondered? You were born in America and lived here your whole life, yet you have a Scottish accent." Her question was out of the blue in some regards, but far later than we'd anticipated she'd ask.

"That's because he didn't live here his whole life."

Her eyes met mine. "What do you mean? I thought—"

I shook my head. "You were led to believe."

"Wait. What?"

"It's time, Laird." While he may believe Maddox, Naughton, and Brodie could keep what he'd told them this morning a secret, they were known to slip up from time to time. I wasn't worried about my daughter being angry like I had been my sons. If she was, she'd get an earful from me about hypocrisy.

"Aye." He stood and kissed Ainsley's forehead before returning to do the same to me. "I'll be excusing myself, then."

I shook my head when he leaned down and his eyes met mine. I put my fingertips on my lips. Fortunately for him, he got the message.

"I've a story to tell you, my darling girl. You best make yourself comfortable."

"Should I be worried?"

"Not at all. I'm going to tell you how your father and I met."

"I already know. You met while he was traveling in Scotland."

"No, lass, we met in Belfast, Northern Ireland." I couldn't tell Ainsley everything Laird had told our sons, because I had no memory of much of that time. I told her what I did know, though.

"That's why you have so much trouble with bronchitis," she said after I'd told her about my time in the German hospital.

"Aye, but it was never that. Not really. Because of my proximity to the explosions, my lungs were damaged enough that I will always be susceptible to respiratory illness."

"There isn't much I can say about that, is there? I kept my relationship with Cristobal a secret too."

I smiled and squeezed her hand. "I had the same thought, daughter."

"But what does this have to do with Da having an accent?"

"I'll get to that part."

Butler Ranch, Paso Robles, California, October 1972

"Da won't really kill him," I said to my mother. "It's just his way of letting Laird know that he expects him to marry me. Given he's already proposed and I said yes, he can rest assured we have every intention of becoming husband and wife."

"You aren't foolish enough to underestimate your father, are you, Sorcha?"

"But, Mum—"

She shook her head. "Mark my words, lass."

It wasn't that I didn't want to get married; I truly did. Just not right away. I wanted to give my body more time to heal, particularly my back and arm, before we were intimate.

At least that's what I told myself. There was another part of me that couldn't help but wonder why we were in such a rush. I was twenty-three years old and needed to figure out what I wanted to do with the rest of my life. The plans I'd had, the work I'd done, I couldn't go back to. Even if PIRA didn't come after me, I could never go undercover again without fear I'd be recognized. My health impacted my work as well. Physically, I wondered if I'd ever be as strong as I was before the blast.

There were other jobs I could do for MI6, but most would be behind a desk, something I swore I'd never do. It was where most women were relegated, and it wasn't for me. But was I prepared to give up my career so soon to become a wife and mother?

There was even a question as to whether or not I could get pregnant or carry a child. When I asked, my doctor told me the only way to find out would be to try. But what if I couldn't give Laird the family I knew he wanted?

He'd confessed as an only child, like I was, he dreamed of having a big family. I'd said I wanted the same thing, but lurking in the back of my mind was the question of whether I could or not.

If it weren't for my father pushing us, Laird and I could take our time and figure out what our life might be like.

His opportunities were endless. Even after walking away mid-mission to stay with me in Germany, neither MI6 nor the CIA had fired him.

"I'll work on my own or not at all," he'd said the night before we were scheduled to get on a plane and fly to the US. He'd been summoned to a meeting at the CIA headquarters, which he immediately refused. He would've had the same request from MI6 if we'd returned to the UK before the States.

One thing I knew without any doubt, though, was that Laird would support me in whatever I decided to do. He'd made that clear whenever we discussed our future.

He'd consulted with me about the security system he put in at the ranch shortly after we arrived, and I found what he did fascinating. Especially when he told me one of his inventions had allowed him to listen in on calls to the Public Protection Agency on Bloody Friday. If he hadn't, he wouldn't have found me at Oxford Street and I probably wouldn't be alive.

I was sitting on a bench near the ranch's vineyards after my conversation with my mother ended. Laird joined me.

"I can reason with him," he began. "Your da assumes we've been…ahem…together, and that's why he's pushing so hard. I can assure him it isn't the case and my reason for sneaking into your bedroom that night was solely because I found I couldn't sleep with you in a different room."

"How have you managed these last days?"

He put his arm around my shoulders. "When at long last my body is tired enough that my eyes drift closed, it's dreams of you that keep me asleep."

"I want to marry you. You know that, yes?"

He smiled. "Because I do know, there is something I'd like to propose. Several things, actually."

"Go on, then."

"Whether we marry here or in Scotland doesn't matter to me. That is my first point. Well, after offering to reason with your father."

"What is your third point?"

"It's more of an offer. One I've received, in fact. I was contacted by MI6, and they're interested in me completing my assigned mission." He'd never let on before now, and I wondered why I'd never asked.

"Will you tell me?"

He laughed. "It isn't as interesting as what you do."

"Did. I don't do it anymore."

"That isn't to say you won't again."

"You are daft if you think so, but thank you. Now get back to MI6."

"My job was to infiltrate PIRA but for the purpose of installing a surveillance system."

"They'd be on to you now."

"Yes and no. First, I don't have to be the one who does it; I can talk other agents through it. Second, there is no means in existence to detect the devices once in place."

I might've questioned him if I hadn't seen his brilliance firsthand with the ranch's security system. However, the last thing I wanted to appear was as a coward, but returning to Belfast seemed too much like tempting fate. Laird knew this, so was he suggesting he go alone? And what of me?

"There must be more to it."

"You could return to Scotland. I'd go with you, obviously."

"Obviously?"

"If I have a hard time sleeping when I'm in the room next door, pray tell how I'd manage with the woman I love in another country."

"What if I can't work again?" I blurted right before putting my head in my hands.

Laird knelt in front of me and moved my hands from my face. "Sorcha, it is only a matter of what you want to do. In Scotland, you can meet with MI6 and discuss your future, if that's what you'd like. If you don't, there are endless other opportunities."

"What opportunities?"

"For one, you and I could work together."

"What would my role be? As your secretary?"

I'd never seen Laird truly cross, with the exception of when I'd refused to follow doctors' orders. Now, though, he seemed angry.

"You are a brilliant strategist. An intelligence mastermind, really. Particularly given your age."

I wasn't sure how to take the age comment, but I'd let it go since he'd called me brilliant and a mastermind. "What would I do, then?"

"You and I would do our part to rid the world of bad guys."

"You make it sound so easy."

"Because it is."

***

"Did you go to Scotland?" Ainsley asked.

"Aye. Once we were married, which was only a few days after we had that conversation. We eloped, in fact."

"How long did you stay?"

"Six years."

Ainsley counted on her fingers. "Until Kade was born?"

"We returned to America when I was pregnant, but more because your grandfather passed, leaving Laird's mother all alone."

"I have a thousand questions, but I can tell you're tired, Ma." She winked. "I'll come back tomorrow, and you can tell me more."

"Come to the house tomorrow. That's where I'll be."

"Of course you will." She bent down to kiss my cheek, then walked toward the door.

"Ainsley, wait. I have a question for you."

"Just one?"

"Aye. Why are you afraid to marry Cristobal?"

"Because he won't ever take me to Scotland."

15

Ainsley

The entire time I listened to my mother, I kept coming back to two things. First, my father loved her unconditionally and unequivocally. Second, he would've followed her to the ends of the earth just to make her happy.

Which led to the third thing I didn't start to think about until after she asked why I was afraid to marry Cristobal. We were nothing like my parents, and that was why I'd ended our engagement. My mother liked to say I'd "put it on hold," but it was more than that.

Between the time he'd proposed and now, my life had changed in ways I never would've imagined. I finished my PhD ahead of schedule, shortly after having a conversation with Naughton on New Year's Day.

"How are things with Butler Ranch Winery?" I'd asked.

"Do you really want to know?"

I'd scrunched my eyes. "Of course I do."

"Now that Maddox and Alex are married and living full-time away from the ranch and working their own winery at Demetria, and Brodie and Peyton are living on Sea Ranch Road and are busy with the new baby, it's becoming harder for Bradley and me to manage it on our own."

"What if I helped?"

Naughton's eyes opened wide. "How?"

"I'm almost done with my doctorate. It isn't like job offers are pouring in. Even if they were, none would matter to me as much as the ranch."

"Um, Ains, didn't you just get engaged?"

I laughed. "Cristobal can work anywhere. He has meetings, but it isn't that hard to commute between here and Palo Alto."

Famous. Last. Words. When I told him my plan, much in the same way Da had told my mother, he was angry I hadn't run this by him before talking with my brother. I explained it was a spur-of-the-moment question, as innocent as asking "How are you?" How was I to know things were so difficult for his wife and him?

"If your family needed you, wouldn't you do everything you could to help?" I'd asked.

"I wouldn't offer to upend my life without discussing it first with the person I'd just agreed to marry."

In the end, I'd been the one to offer a compromise. I'd work three to four days a week at Butler Ranch and spend the rest of the week with him in Palo Alto. Like everything else in life, it hadn't turned out to be that simple.

Cris worked so much that I found myself resenting being there with nothing to do when I could be home, working like he was.

Home. That was another point of contention. Palo Alto was where I'd gone to school. I'd never seen myself spending the rest of my life there. Cris, on the other hand, saw no reason to move back to the Central Coast.

Feeling like I was the only one making any sacrifices, every minute I spent alone turned my resentment into anger. Finally, when we talked about Thanksgiving and he said he wasn't sure he wanted to spend it with our families, I lost my temper.

"Last year, it was all you could think about. You *broke up with me* over it. Was it just so I'd come clean about us? You got what you wanted, and now it doesn't matter anymore?"

When he responded by saying I was being melo-dramatic, I packed my overnight bag and left. Before I closed the door behind me, I threw my engagement ring at him.

He'd apologized—over the phone—and asked me to come back so we could talk about it. I didn't bother to suggest that if I really mattered to him, he'd come to me instead. If he couldn't figure that much out on his own, did I really want to be married to him?

When he called earlier to tell me he would be here in the morning, I was elated. Stupidly thinking he was coming to talk about us. Instead, I quickly learned he was accompanying Stanford's medical director here as a favor to my parents. The man had invented an oxygen delivery device that would allow my mother to leave the hospital earlier than her doctor recommended.

Sure, I was happy about that part. Sorcha Butler would be monstrous if she had to spend Christmas away from her family. More, we'd be lost without her.

I'd spent so much of the last few months feeling angry, and I was tired of it. I wanted to enjoy the holidays with my family, the first where we'd all be together in years and years. I had nieces and nephews to spoil and brothers and sisters-in-law that I never got to spend enough time with. My sister, Skye, and I met for lunch at least once a week, but that was just her and the kids. I rarely got to see her husband, Mac, and he was one of my favorite people.

On the drive home, I vowed not to let Cristobal Avila spoil Christmas for me. Of course I was sad—heartbroken, really—but it was time for me to move on. Maybe next year I'd have a new man in my life to celebrate with. If not, I was happy to play my role as aunty. If this was how my life was supposed to be, I could live it happily. Just because I was the only one in our family still single, didn't mean I needed to marry someone I'd be unhappy with.

I was in the winery office the next morning, processing Christmas wine shipments when my cell phone rang with a call from Cris. I thought about not answering it, but if it was anything to do with my mother, I wanted to know.

"Hi," I said.

"Where are you?"

"At work. How's my mom?"

"I thought you'd be here."

"I had no reason to be, but would you answer my question about my mother?"

"She's improving. Her oxygen levels got better overnight, and with the HHFC cannula, there is less risk they will dip to dangerous levels again."

"What about the pneumonia?" It was what had landed her in the hospital in the first place.

"It's improving as well. I doubt she'll be able to come home today, but if her condition continues to improve, she'll be able to tomorrow."

"Thanks for the update. I'll come see her this afternoon. Bye, Cris."

"Ainsley, wait."

I tapped my fingers on my desk. "What?"

"I was hoping we could talk."

"Yeah? Well, I'm all talked out. Thanks for helping my mother. Take care." I ended the call before he could charm me into yet another conversation that ended with me agreeing to whatever he wanted, like I always did. I'd followed the man around like a lost puppy since I was an adolescent. I'd soon be twenty-seven years old. It was time to stop following and lead my own life.

I wasn't surprised when Cris wasn't there when I got to the hospital a few hours later. Why would he have been? He probably had to rush back with Dr. Monroe, since that was the only reason he'd come.

"There's a bonny lass," said my father when I walked into the room. I stepped into his loving embrace, so thankful for my parents.

"We missed you earlier, Ainsley," said my mother. Even through the oxygen mask, I could see her sour look.

"I was working."

When she shook her head and looked away, I came close to losing my temper. Before I did, I stepped closer and kissed her forehead.

"I'll see you tomorrow at home." I turned on my heel and walked out, hoping my father wouldn't follow. If anyone could guilt me into staying, it would be him. I breathed a sigh of relief when the elevator door closed behind me.

I was looking at my phone when I stepped off, and nearly ran into someone. "Sorry," I muttered without looking up, just shifting out of the way.

"Ainsley?"

I stopped dead in my tracks. "Cris? What are you doing here?"

"I've been waiting for you. I don't know how you got past me."

I shrugged. "Don't know. Anyway—"

"Wait. Don't leave. Can we please talk?"

I sighed and shook my head. "I don't see the point. You made your position clear, and while I went along with it for a little while, I can't any longer. I never dreamed I'd say this, but we want two different things in life. The best thing is for us to go our separate ways."

"Is there someone else?"

My mouth dropped open. "Did you really just ask me that? We broke up three weeks ago." Something occurred to me that made my gut clench. "Is that why you won't leave Palo Alto? Has there been someone else the whole time?"

"You can't be serious."

"No? They say when one person accuses the other of something totally ludicrous, it's because they're doing it themselves."

He shook his head and looked at the floor. "I would never cheat on you, and I'm sorry I asked."

"Apology accepted. Now, if there's nothing else."

"There's so much more. Can we please go somewhere and talk? *Please*."

"Know this. I'm not going back to the way we were. I can't. If that's what you're hoping for, don't waste both our time."

"That isn't what I want."

"I'm sorry to say this, but I don't believe you."

I could see the hurt in his eyes, but I couldn't let it sway me. Even if it did, it would only be temporary. Soon we'd be back in the same place we were now.

"We can talk." It was as much as I'd give. "Follow me." Rather than risk going to Butler Ranch or anywhere else we could truly be alone, I led him to the hospital chapel.

"Here?" he asked when I opened the door and motioned him inside.

"Or nowhere."

He sighed and held the door for me instead.

We sat in the front pew in silence long enough that I began to think he was waiting for me to go first, but I'd already said everything I intended to.

He sat forward, put his elbows on his knees, and dropped his head. "I probably shouldn't say this in a chapel, but I fucked up, Ains. I handled things wrong."

I couldn't help myself. I laughed. "I think God has probably heard the word before. Especially here." I was sure there had been many people who cursed God's name in this place after hearing their loved one was sick or dying.

"I got so wrapped up in my work, I lost sight of you. I won't let that happen again. But we're so close to truly hitting on something that could dramatically increase the lifespan of the human race."

I waited to see if he'd say anything else. After several more minutes of silence, I stood and walked to the door.

"Tell me this, Cris. What's the point of living forever if you don't have love in your life?" I let the chapel door close behind me.

16

Cristobal

I let her go. What choice did I have other than giving in to what she wanted? And that, I couldn't do. There was no way I could leave Palo Alto unless I built an entirely new lab in Paso Robles. Even if I could, it would take months to construct, and then the likelihood the scientists I worked with would agree to relocate was nonexistent. Santa Clara County was the hotbed of genetic research. It was especially true the closer to Stanford a facility was.

Did she really expect me to walk away from something that could literally change the world? For what? So she could help her family sell more wine? The disparity in the kind of work we did was ridiculous. How could she not see that?

At first I thought she was just being stubborn, but today it seemed like more than that. For the first time, I believed things might really be over for us. I hadn't thought that even when she threw her ring at me.

I loved Ainsley Butler. I had for as long as I could remember. I didn't want to lose her, but she was asking too much of me. I couldn't give up my work. If she really loved me, understood me, she wouldn't ask me to.

17

Sorcha

"Tha mi ceart gu leòr," I said to my husband when he scolded me for being in the kitchen.

"You are *not* fine. You are recovering and at home. Do you really want to end up back in the hospital on Christmas Eve?"

"Na bi gòrach. Now be on your way. I'm sure you have plenty to attend to after spending so much time at the hospital with me—*Laird*!" I shrieked when he scooped me into his arms and carried me from the kitchen. "You'll hurt yourself!"

"I'm not so old and feeble that I cannot toss you over my shoulder and make you behave. If you keep this up, I'll find the paddle we used to use on the bairns."

I started to giggle. "I'd take your threat more seriously if I was actually over your shoulder."

"Don't tempt me, woman."

"I'm serious. Put me down," I demanded when he got to the bottom of the staircase.

"Will you promise on my life to go upstairs and lie down?"

"I cannot lie down. It's almost Christmas and nothing is done. You haven't even decorated—"

He stomped up the stairs with me in his arms. "You are supposed to have your oxygen with you at all times." He set me on our bed and handed me the mask.

"I'm feeling fine. No trouble breathing whatsoever. You're overreacting."

His eyes scrunched. *"Put it on, Sorcha!"*

"There is no need to raise your voice with me—"

Laird held the mask up to my nose and mouth. "Put it on, or I will take you straight back to the hospital."

He surprised me by gathering me in his arms as soon as I did as he'd asked. I pulled back to look into his eyes. Something felt different.

"Laird?"

"Do you have any idea how frightened I am of losing you? *Any idea*?"

"You aren't going—"

"You were in intensive care, my love. Your oxygen levels plummeted far enough that the medical staff believed you could die. How can you so easily disregard my feelings?"

"Your feelings?" I said, perhaps too quietly for him to hear through my mask.

"Yes, Sorcha. My feelings."

My eyes filled with tears when his did.

"I have loved you practically my whole life. There are days I pray I die before you because I don't know how I could live without you. At the same time, I pray I don't because I can't stand the idea of you being alone with no one to make sure you take care of yourself." He broke down then, tears streaming down his cheeks. He took my hand and put it on his heart. "Make no mistake. I love our children and grandchildren, but know this. My heart beats for you, my love. It has gone on beating for forty-six years just for you. Please do not be so careless with it."

It was easy to argue with him when I thought my actions only affected me. Hearing how I was hurting him stunned me. I moved the mask from my face. "I'm sorry, my love. I'll not do it again." I put it back and rested my head on the pillow.

Laird lay beside me, his arm around my waist and his leg between mine. I rested my head on his shoulder, and we both slept.

When I woke again, the sun was setting. Laird was still asleep, but his hand had moved from my waist to my breast, where it often rested when we slept.

We might be considered old by some people's standards, but our sex life was as good now as it had been in all the years we'd been married.

As worried as I'd been about our first time together, Laird had always made me feel like the most beautiful and desirable woman in the world, not in spite of my scars but because of them.

We'd made a family out of our love for each other, and while those days were long since past for us, intimacy between us never wavered.

I inwardly giggled at what his reaction would be if I put my hand on the zipper of his trousers. I'd likely get another scolding. Maybe he'd even paddle me.

"Sorcha," he warned when I couldn't stop myself from giggling outwardly. I knew he wasn't truly annoyed when his fingers toyed with my nipple.

I moved the oxygen mask. "*Dinnae* start something you won't finish, husband."

"When have I not finished? Now, put the mask back on."

18

Ainsley

"I heard Cris is in town," said Naughton, coming in the day after our mom came home and plopping himself in the chair by my desk.

"Was."

"Sorry, Ains."

I shrugged. "Don't be. It's better we realized it wasn't going to work between us now rather than after we got married."

"You're sure it's reached that point?"

"Positive."

He got up and walked to the window. "Huh."

"Huh, what?"

"I think you're wrong." He smiled and walked out of my office.

When I got up to close the door he'd left open, Cris was about to cross the threshold. "What are you doing here? We said everything—"

He backed me up against the wall and pressed his body against mine. "Maybe you did, but I haven't."

I tried to resist falling into his kiss, but it was pointless. Nothing ever felt more right than when our bodies were joined together, even if it was just our lips.

"I thought you left," I said when he rested his forehead against mine.

"You left. I stayed in the chapel. I'm not sure how long I sat there before your dad joined me."

I got that my parents loved and wanted the best for me, but the time had come for them to stop interfering. "I'm sorry."

"Don't be. We ended up talking for a couple of hours. I asked if he needed to get back to Sorcha, but he said my sister and Maddox were with her and that Brodie, Peyton, Kade, and Merrigan were on their way."

"What did you talk about?" I asked as he nuzzled my neck.

"He told me the story of how he and your mom really met and how terrified he was of losing her. Both then and now."

"He loves her so much."

"When he got up to leave, he told me to visit my mom and ask her about my dad."

"Did you?"

"Yes."

I tried to wriggle out of his arms, but he wouldn't let go.

"Do you want to know what she said?"

"What?"

"I asked how she'd feel if I told her she could live another hundred years, at least, and instead of her body aging, it would go in reverse."

"And?"

"She put her hand on my cheek and told me she loved my siblings and me very much, but not enough to live another hundred years without my father." He brushed my lips with his. "She believes he's waiting for her in heaven."

"Cris, I—"

"I heard what you said, Ainsley. Not right away, but I spent most of the past two days thinking about whether I'd want to live forever if it meant I'd have to do it without love—without you."

"I can't do what you want me to. I can't live in Palo Alto and do nothing while you're at work hours on end."

"I don't want you to do that."

When I wriggled again, he let me go.

"What *do* you want me to do? Get a job up there? I can't do that either. I want to work here, at Butler Ranch. I know you can't understand that, but this place is just as important to me as your research is to you. Especially now. For almost two years, I believed my brother was dead. I mourned him. I figured out how to go on without him, but when he came back, I promised myself I'd never take my family for granted ever again."

"I don't know what the answer is, Ains, but I want us to figure out a way we can be together and both of us able to continue doing what's important to us."

"We tried that. It didn't work."

He took my hands in his. "You tried. I did nothing. That's why it didn't work. I want to be the one to try now. I want us to be together. To spend the rest of our lives together."

"I can't marry you until I'm sure."

"I can accept that."

I shook my head. Could my heart handle it if I agreed and nothing changed? "I don't know how to do this."

He wrapped his arms around my waist and pulled my body into his. "I have a couple of ideas."

I closed my eyes and took a deep breath. "What?"

"We get a place of our own down here."

"Where?"

"I'll show you if you'll take a ride with me."

"Cris—"

"Come with me, Ainsley. That's all I'm asking for right now."

I prayed he would take me exactly where he did. I'd fallen in love with Alex's house at the beach last year when we stayed there for Christmas.

"She'll rent it to us?"

"She doesn't own it anymore."

I grabbed the porch railing and took a deep breath. "Who does?"

"We do. Or we will by the end of the day. I just need you to agree to come with me to sign the escrow papers."

"I don't know if I can afford this."

"I'm putting up the money for it, Ains. There's no risk on your part. It'll be as much yours as it is mine, but it's my commitment to live here. Be here. With you."

"You don't have to do this. Buy it, I mean."

"You're wrong. I do have to. It's a start. I know there's so much more for us to figure out, but I am trying my damnedest to prove to you that I want to."

I studied him, looking for any sign of hesitation but saw none.

"Well?"

"What time do we have to be there?"

He checked his phone. "We have three hours."

"Do you have the key?"

Cris took it out of his pocket. "Right here."

"Maybe we should go inside."

"Yeah? And do what?"

"I have a couple of ideas."

19

Sorcha

All four of my daughters-in-law and one of my daughters were in the kitchen of the main house, preparing food for Christmas week. With all of our children staying on the ranch with their families, we would need several meals' worth. Well, I wasn't sure about all of our children—we hadn't heard from Ainsley. I asked Naught, and he said she hadn't been at work either.

I thought my Laird would insist I stay in the cottage we'd moved into after Naughton and Bradley moved into this place, but he didn't say a word. My guess was he gave everyone else stern orders about what I was allowed to do and not.

"Did you hear the news?" Alex said, sitting down on the arm of my chair.

With as many kids as we had, who knew? "Which news is that?"

"Cris and Ainsley bought my beach house."

If my arse hadn't been firmly planted in my chair, I might've fallen over. "What's this now?"

"I'm not surprised they haven't told anyone. If it wasn't my house, I'm sure I wouldn't have known either. I think they're trying to figure things out for themselves before they share it with everyone."

I leaned closer to her so everyone didn't overhear. "Is that where they've been, then?"

"Oh, definitely. I'm pretty sure they donated all of my old furniture to the assistance league and have been busy filling it with new stuff. They called to ask if I wanted any of it, but Mad and I have too much stuff in our house as it is."

"My word," I said under my breath. I'd figured Ainsley was off on her own, not wanting to be around all her happily married siblings when she was in so much pain. That, I could understand. I'd never dreamed what Alex had just told me.

"That's where Mad is now. He and Brodie are helping Cris paint while Ains watches Coco and Kismet."

"I'd wondered where those two were." Bradley and Naughton's son, Charlie, and Kade and Merrigan's son, Laird, were both in their portable cribs, napping. Skye's husband, Mac, had kept their two, Spencer and Kade, with him today so she could be here.

"There's a beautiful woman," said my own Laird, coming in from the vineyards with Naught and Kade.

When Alex got up to return to the kitchen, my husband sat on the ottoman in front of me.

"Ainsley and Cris bought her beach house," I whispered. "I *dinnae* have any idea."

He nodded. "I was just about to ask you out onto the porch to tell you that myself."

"What do you make of it? It seemed hopeless between them."

"It might've been me threatening to kill him like your da did to me."

He winked and I smacked him. "You didn't."

"You're right, but we did talk."

"You said, but not about what."

He leaned forward and kissed me. "The power of the love of a woman."

20

I went out to ask Ainsley about the color she wanted for the bathroom, but stopped and watched her with her nieces, Kismet and Coco—who was my niece too.

Ainsley's brother Brodie and his wife, Peyton, were one-year-old Kismet's parents. Coco, Alex and Maddox's daughter, was five months old.

Was Ainsley ready for us to start a family? As wrapped up as I'd been with my research, there were so many things like that I'd never stopped to consider.

What about our wedding? Not that I'd push her on when that would happen. She'd said she wouldn't be ready to take that step until she was sure things would get better between us.

But when she was ready, what would she want? A big wedding at Butler Ranch, or maybe even to get married here on Moonstone Beach? And what about a honeymoon? We'd never talked about that either.

"Everything okay?" she asked.

I realized I'd been staring right through her. "Just thinking what a good mom you'll be someday."

"Get out."

"Seriously. I mean, if that's something you still want."

"Do you?"

I came over and sat next to her on the grass. While it was warm today, both babies were bundled up in sweaters, jackets, and hats, lying on one blanket with another on top of them.

"Kismet was wearing me out until I told her I needed her help getting her cousin to stop crying. Before I knew it, they were both asleep. Do you think I should take them inside?"

"The paint fumes aren't good for them."

"Maybe I should take them to the ranch."

"Their dads are here. You could ask them what they think."

"Right. See? I'm not that good at this. I'm fine once they're a little older, like Spencer, but the baby thing rattles me."

I laughed. "Rattles you?"

"I wish I could say I did that on purpose, but I didn't. So, you never answered me about whether you want to have a family. I mean, we've talked about it in the abstract."

"I do…"

She scooted over and put her head on my shoulder. God, I'd missed feeling her body next to mine.

"But?"

"I blame lab brain. Too many complex thoughts and ideas have made me unable to process simple things like how I feel."

"Is that a thing? I mean is that what it's called? Lab brain?"

"Not officially, but it does seem as though I've stepped out of an alternate universe and back into one I like a lot better."

"You've taken on a lot in the last two years, Cris. I remember after you left the hospital, you said you'd be working less, have more regular hours."

I leaned back and looked up at the sky. When was the last time I'd sat on the grass and did that? I couldn't remember. "I'm sorry, Ains."

"I am too."

"I feel like I lost sight of my own life, trying to extend the lives of others."

Back when we were both still in school, we had a rhythm. And while our classes were very different, particularly when I started my residency, we still both knew what to expect. "I misjudged everything."

She leaned up and kissed my cheek.

"Thanks for that."

Coco started to cry, which woke Kismet up. I scooped the littlest one into my arms while Ainsley lay beside Kismet and whispered something I couldn't hear.

"Tows!" she said, pointing up that the sky.

"Tows?"

"It's what she calls cows," Ainsley explained. I looked up at where she pointed. "Cloud cow, but it's gone now."

I got up and bounced Coco, rubbing her back until she settled down.

"Cris?"

"Yeah?"

"You'll make a good dad someday too."

"Hey, kids," said Alex, getting out of the car I hadn't seen her pull into the driveway. "Gotta warn you; I kind of let the cat out of the bag on the house."

I raised a brow. "Kind of?"

She went around to the trunk and got out two baskets. "From Sorcha. Lunch for you and lunch for my man and his brother."

I glanced at Ainsley, who didn't appear affected by Alex's cat-out-of-the-bag statement.

"Hope you're not mad," my sister said, taking her baby from my arms. "And by you, I don't mean you. I mean Ainsley."

"Me?" She looked surprised. "Why would I be mad? The more you tell her, the less I have to."

Both women laughed.

"I've always liked her. Even when she used to spy on Maddox and me."

"I wondered if you knew I was."

"Yeah, we had that secret thing going on a long while by then. You weren't exactly a super sleuth, if you know what I mean. Not like Sorcha. How wild is that, by the way?"

"I thought I heard the sexiest voice in the world, although not calling out my name like I would've preferred," said Maddox, coming out the front door and giving my sister the kind of kiss I wished I could lay on Ainsley right now. I sat back down beside her and nuzzled her neck. "What do you say we spend the night somewhere romantic tonight?"

"What's more romantic than my beach house?" said my sister, eavesdropping pain in the ass that she was.

"Maybe they want to get away from paint fumes," said Maddox, taking Coco from Alex like she had from me.

"You could take her to that place Brix did for the auction. The one with tree houses."

"Tree houses? Might be a little cold for that." I kissed the back of Ainsley's neck, wishing our siblings would take their children and leave, so we could be alone. "Run along and mind your business, Al."

"Wait. Did you say Brix was in the bachelor auction? We completely forgot about the Wicked Winemakers' Ball this year."

It was something Ainsley looked forward to every year, and I doubted she'd forgotten about it. I was the one who'd dropped the so-called ball on that one.

"Sure enough, and we made twice as much for the Children's Hospital than we did last year. Mostly thanks to him."

I glared up at my sister.

"*And* that's a story for another time." She looked over at her husband. "You ready to get out of here, Mad?"

He rolled his neck. "Thought you'd never ask."

"Is it quitting time?" asked Brodie, coming out the front door like Maddox had.

"If it ain't, you're on your own, bro."

"See you back at the ranch," said Alex, picking up Kismet and handing her to Brodie.

"I thought we were going home," whined Maddox.

"We are. And after you shower, we're going to see your family."

He stuck his lower lip out. "Right after my shower?"

I felt the same way he did. If her two brothers and my sister didn't hurry up and get out of here, I would toss Ainsley over my shoulder, carry her in the house, and lock the door behind us. I couldn't keep my hands off her another minute.

"Don't forget, dinner is at six," she shouted from the window as Maddox drove their car away.

"Do you want to go, Ains?" I asked.

"Sounds like we're expected. Would you mind?"

"Not at all."

She didn't look happy, though.

"We don't have to. We can look into the tree house idea."

"It isn't that." She looked down at her hand absent-mindedly and rubbed her ring finger.

"Are you missing something? Because I know where it is."

Her eyes met mine. "Where?"

"Right here." I took my hand out of my pocket and opened my palm.

"Would you mind?" she asked, resting her left hand on my arm.

"Nothing would make me happier." I slipped the engagement ring back on her finger, then winked. "Except maybe going inside and getting you naked."

"As long as you're naked too."

I reached behind me and pulled my shirt over my head. "Way ahead of you," I said, racing her to the front door.

21

Ainsley

"Did you tell anyone we were broken up?" I asked Cris on our way to the ranch.

"Only my mom, but she already knew."

"Sorry."

"What for?"

"I'm sure my mother told her. Or my father."

Cris smiled and shook his head. "I think she knew the minute I walked into her house."

"Think we'll be like that?"

He squeezed my hand. "When we're parents?"

"Yeah."

"I can say for certain you will be. I'm not sure I'm as aware of the world around me as you are."

"Lab brain."

He laughed. "What about you?"

"Just my parents and only when my mother was in the hospital."

"Think they told everyone?"

I raised a brow. "They're better at keeping secrets than we are."

We were the last ones to arrive, and when we walked in, Skye and Mac's daughter Spencer raced toward us. "Auntie Ainsley," she yelped, jumping into my arms.

"Spence," scolded her father when I groaned.

"She's okay." I kissed her nose. "How old are you now, anyway? Sixteen?"

She giggled. "I'm five, and you saw me last week."

"I think what she's trying to say is you're heavy." Mac took my niece out of my arms and kissed my cheek. "You look radiant tonight, Ains. Being in love suits you."

"She told, didn't she?" I looked around the room for my mother.

"Glad to see that back on your finger," he whispered, looking down at my hand. "Your sister noticed it was missing."

"She didn't say anything."

Mac winked. "You didn't either."

"I was hoping we'd see you tonight," said Kade, putting his arm around my shoulders and shaking Cris' hand. "You've made yourself scarce these last couple of days."

"We bought Alex's beach house," I blurted.

"Congratulations! I hope that means there will be a wedding in the near future?"

"We're working on it," said Cris, hugging me close.

"The house in Montecito is available. Although there are two wineries I can think of that would work beautifully for a ceremony and a reception."

"We could always do what you did and elope."

Kade looked over his shoulder at where Merrigan sat talking to our mother, who held baby Laird on her lap. "I wouldn't recommend it. I'm still on Ma's shit list for that stunt."

"She and Da eloped."

He nodded. "I heard they told everyone the real story about how they met."

"Shh. I'm not sure Skye knows yet." I motioned to our sister.

"Merrigan said Ma told her, Skye, Bradley, and Alex today."

"Good. I hope that's the end of the secrets."

"There might still be a story or two left to tell," said Merrigan, walking up behind my brother. "Hello, Ainsley. How are you?"

We cheek kissed. "I'm well. It's good to see you." I looked around the room. "I can't remember the last time we were all together for Christmas." My cheeks turned pink when I realized one person was missing. "I'm sorry, Kade. I forgot Quinn and her husband are traveling."

He smiled and looked at his wife. "No more secrets, right?" she whispered.

Kade leaned forward. "I wanted to surprise Ma. She and Mercer will be here on Christmas Eve."

My eyes filled with happy tears. "That will be really wonderful."

I looked up at Cris, who appeared lost in thought.

"Where did you go?" I asked once Kade and his wife walked away.

"Nowhere." He sighed, took my hand in his, and led me to the side of the room. "I want you to know how much I love you, Ainsley, and how thankful I am that you gave me another chance."

"What were you thinking about? I know that wasn't it."

When he shook his head, I pulled him out the door and onto the front porch. "Tell me. *Now.*"

"I promised I wouldn't push. As long as you are wearing that ring again, I can wait."

I crossed my arms and tapped my foot. "*I'm* waiting. Something about our whole family being together made you sad. What?"

He looked away, and I put my palm on his cheek. "I'm sorry. Is it that your father isn't here?"

He grabbed my hand and kissed it. "I wish I could lie and say that's what it is." He sighed. "It's just that all of your family is here this year, and so is mine."

"I see."

"Don't be mad, Ains. I wouldn't have said anything if you hadn't made me."

22

Sorcha

"I never dreamed such a day would happen," I said when Laird and I crawled in bed after saying good night to our children and grandchildren, who were still gathered in the main house.

He gathered me in his arms. "We have three more days ahead that will be just like this."

"We're missing one, you know."

"Aye. I'm sure Kade is sadder than we are that Quinn won't be with us."

"It seems your talk with Cristobal worked wonders."

"I cannot take credit for him convincing our daughter to put his ring back on her finger."

"Do you think they'll ever marry?"

Laird chuckled. "I'm certain of it. Sooner than we expect, is my guess."

I sat up and leaned over him. "If you know something—"

He held up his hands. "I promise I know no more than you do."

I lay back down and put my hand on his heart.

"Sorcha, my love?"

"Yes, my darling?"

"Put the oxygen mask back on."

23

Ainsley

Christmas Eve

"I am a damned good secret keeper," said Alex.

"That isn't why I asked you to come with me."

She put her hand on her hip. "Why did you?"

"You're the first person Cristobal and I told that we were together. It seems fitting you'd be here today."

She laughed. "I see what you did there."

"How did it go?" Cris asked when she dropped me off at the beach house.

I bit my lower lip.

"If you're having second thoughts…"

"I'm not."

"Did you tell your parents we'd be arriving late tonight?"

I shook my head. "Alex said she'd tell them."

"Is she taking care of everything else?"

"Like no one else would be able to. Everything will have to go like clockwork, or this won't happen."

"It'll happen."

Five hours later, I stood just inside the entrance to the wine caves. Cristobal's family and mine, most of whom had no idea what was about to happen, were gathered, waiting in the main room.

"Ready?" asked my father, joining me when the string quartet Alex had arranged for began to play Pachelbel's Canon in D.

"Never more so. Is Cris?"

"Oh, yes."

When my father escorted me through the door, the din of conversation fell silent as all eyes turned to me.

My gaze met my mother's first and then Cris' mom's, both of whom had tears in their eyes.

Like I'd asked only Alex, Cris had asked just one man to stand with him. It meant the world to me that it was my brother Kade.

Those gathered stepped aside, creating a pathway for my father and I to walk. Once we reached the front of the room, he kissed my cheek and took a step back.

Cristobal held out his hand, and I stepped forward to join him in front of the minister who'd agreed to marry us between Christmas Eve services.

"Please be seated," the man said when the quartet stopped playing and chairs appeared. Another miracle Alex had managed to pull off.

"You are breathtaking," said Cris, leaning over to kiss me.

When the minister cleared his throat, Cris kissed my cheek instead.

"Dearly beloved," he began.

It seemed as though it was only moments later when he pronounced us husband and wife and told us that *now* we could kiss.

"Ladies and gentlemen, I am thrilled to present Mr. and Mrs. Butler-Avila," shouted Alex.

Our families cheered and the quartet began to play again when we turned and raised our clasped hands in the air.

My mother and Lucia stood and raced toward us, tears now streaming down their faces. I hugged them both and turned around when I felt another hand on my shoulder.

"As you know, I'm the one who picked out your name, little one," said my oldest brother, who also had tears in his eyes.

"And Maddox said you'd hold me and refuse to let me go."

"That's right. Until tonight. Cris is the only man I'd let Da give you away to."

I laughed through my tears. "I'm so glad you're here."

"Later, after we've had more wine, we'll get Merrigan to tell you the story of how she made sure I would be."

Cris and I stood together as, one by one, every member of both our families came forward to congratulate us.

"Where's Quinn?" I whispered to Alex when she brought me another glass of wine and asked if we were ready for dinner to be served.

Rather than answer, she picked up a fork and tapped it repeatedly against the side of her wineglass.

For the second time, a hush fell over the room as Kade approached with my niece, his daughter, a woman I hadn't known existed until a year ago. She'd insisted on watching our ceremony from outside the room so she didn't disrupt it.

"I think we should hold off on dinner for a little while," I said to Alex, watching as my mother and father were the first to greet their granddaughter and her husband.

I stood next to my own husband, overwhelmed by the love and joy surrounding us.

"Are you ready for your surprise?" he asked.

"You're actually going to tell me where we're going on our honeymoon?"

"Only if you want me to."

"Wait until tomorrow. It can be my Christmas present."

24

Sorcha

I looked around the room at our sons and daughters, the youngest now—finally—happily married. Everyone was here and would still be in the morning. Husbands, wives, and children would lay their heads to rest in the house that Broderick Butler built for his wife, Analise, and where Laird brought me forty-six years ago to keep me safe after saving my life.

At times, I'd wondered what would've happened had he not been at the Oxford Street Station that awful day. Or if he hadn't found me. But the idea of it was too painful to consider.

The good Lord had seen to it he was there and further blessed us with the gift of each of our dear children. From the two of us were born not just six, but generations to come. Soon, we would have our first great-grandchild, our beloved Quinn had announced tonight.

It was one of many gifts Laird and I received this evening and would continue to receive tomorrow.

As I held each of my grandchildren in my arms and looked into their eyes, I saw their parents in them. Those were the greatest gifts of all—Kade, Maddox, Naughton, Skye, Brodie, and Ainsley. Our blessed miracles.

"Oh, but to be able to read your mind, my love," said my dear husband, coming to sit beside me.

"I was counting our blessings."

"They are many, aren't they?"

I turned to him and put my palm on his cheek. "All because of you. *Shàbhail thu mo bheatha.*"

"Shh, now, my precious Rua. Everything went as it should. My only regret was not being able to spare you from the pain you've suffered."

"It's worth it since it brought me you."

"We need to rest. Christmas morning is nigh upon us. How many times did we rise before dawn to make sure all the gifts were under the tree, the stockings were full, and a hearty breakfast ready when our bairns came running down the stairs?"

"Many more to come, I pray."

"Aye. Many, many more."

I rested my head on his shoulder. "Take me to bed, husband."

"Those words have always been my dreams come true."

25

Laird

I've heard it said that Christmas is for children, but there is no greater joy for a parent beyond seeing their sons and daughters happy. Be it from a bicycle or baby doll, a marriage, or a family of their own.

There was one more gift that had yet to be opened, and I was anxiously awaiting the look on my youngest daughter's face when she did.

"What's this?" I heard her ask Cristobal when he handed her an envelope. The previously noisy room went silent.

"Your surprise. Open it."

I knew what was inside, as did my wife, but we still held our breath, waiting for her reaction.

"Oh my God," she said, pulling the itinerary out and unfolding it.

"What is it?" shouted little Spencer.

"A ticket."

"To where?" she asked.

Ainsley looked from her husband, to me, then to her mother. "Cristobal is taking me to Scotland."

Sorcha's eyes closed, and she nodded her head. "Aye, I never doubted he would."

Keep reading for a sneak peek
at the first book in the
Wicked Winemakers Central Coast
First Label Series—
Brix's Bid

He became her champion.
She stole his heart.
Between high-stakes intrigue and
small-town charm, can their love
overcome the divide of two worlds?

BRIX

I've always been focused on my family's business empire, until Addison Reagan captured my heart. When she's falsely accused of murder, I will stop at nothing to protect her and uncover the truth. As I find myself falling deeper in love, I must navigate the complexities of my wealthy world and Addison's small-town life. Can I find a way to merge the two without losing the woman who's become my perfect match?

ADDISON

I've spent my life working hard and dreaming of a better future. When I meet the handsome and wealthy Brix Avila, I discover a new kind of yearning—for love and belonging. As I grapple with family secrets and false accusations, I'm torn between my loyalty to my mother and my growing feelings for Brix. Can I find the courage to trust in love and build a future that's sweeter than I ever imagined?

Prologue

Brix

"One of our own is in trouble."

After my blunt statement, the wine cellar grew eerily quiet. Every one of the men of Los Caballeros Society—not named for my family's winery as everyone assumed, but rather the other way around—moved closer to the table.

The secret society dating back to our grandfathers' grandfathers only met when necessary, when someone needed our help. We were brothers—some by blood, some not, but brothers all the same.

"Who?" My uncle Trystan Avila spoke first. "All nine of us are here."

I dipped my chin in acknowledgment. "Fair enough." I steepled my fingers on the large table in front of me. "It's Addison Reagan."

The three men at the table who were my brothers by blood, Cru, Snapper, and Kick, looked at me with wide eyes. "What happened?" asked the latter.

"She's been arrested," my best friend Ridge answered, saving me from revealing the emotion the words would evoke.

I swallowed and finished the sentence. "For murder."

About the Author

USA Today best-selling author Heather Slade writes shamelessly sexy, edge-of-your seat romantic suspense.

She gave herself the gift of writing a book for her own birthday one year. Sixty-plus books later (and counting), she's having the time of her life.

The women Slade writes are self-confident, strong, with wills of their own, and hearts as big as the Colorado sky. The men are sublimely sexy, seductive alphas who rise to the challenge of capturing the sweet soul of a woman whose heart they'll hold in the palm of their hand forever. Add in a couple of neck-snapping twists and turns, a page-turning mystery, and a swoon-worthy HEA, and you'll be holding one of her books in your hands.

She loves to hear from her readers. You can contact her at heather@heatherslade.com

To keep up with her latest news and releases, please visit her website at www.heatherslade.com to sign up for her newsletter.

MORE FROM AUTHOR HEATHER SLADE

ROMANTIC SUSPENSE

K19 SECURITY SOLUTIONS TEAM ONE
Razor's Edge
Gunner's Redemption
Mistletoe's Magic
Mantis' Desire
Dutch's Salvation

K19 SECURITY SOLUTIONS TEAM TWO
Striker's Choice
Monk's Fire
Halo's Oath
Tackle's Honor
Onyx's Awakening

K19 SHADOW OPERATIONS TEAM ONE
Code Name: Ranger
Code Name: Diesel
Code Name: Wasp
Code Name: Cowboy
Code Name: Mayhem

K19 ALLIED INTELLIGENCE TEAM ONE
Code Name: Ares
Code Name: Cayman
Code Name: Poseidon
Code Name: Zeppelin
Code Name: Magnet

K19 ALLIED INTELLIGENCE TEAM TWO
Code Name: Puck
Code Name: Michelangelo
Code Name: Typhon
Code Name: Hornet
Code Name: Reaper

K19 GENESIS CONSORTIUM TEAM ONE
Blackjack's Ascent
Dagger's Shield
Sundance's Trail
Nomad's Compass
Preacher's Decree

K19 SENTINEL CYBER TEAM ONE
Code Name: Admiral
Code Name: Dante
Code Name: Grit
Code Name: Tank
Code Name: Atticus

K19 SENTINEL CYBER TEAM TWO
Code Name: Kodiak
Code Name: Paragon
Code Name: Vex
Code Name: Shredder
Code Name: Jagger

PROTECTORS UNDERCOVER TEAM ONE
Undercover Agent
Undercover Emissary
Undercover Savior
Undercover Infidel
Undercover Shadow

ROYAL AGENTS OF MI6
Make Me Shiver
Drive Me Wilder
Feel My Pinch
Chase My Shadow
Find My Angel

THE INVINCIBLES TEAM ONE
Code Name: Deck
Code Name: Edge
Code Name: Grinder
Code Name: Rile
Code Name: Smoke

THE INVINCIBLES TEAM TWO
Code Name: Buck
Code Name: Irish
Code Name: Saint
Code Name: Hammer
Code Name: Rip

THE UNSTOPPABLES TEAM ONE
Code Name: Fury
Code Name: Merried

MORE FROM AUTHOR HEATHER SLADE

WINE COUNTRY ROMANCE

BUTLER RANCH
Kade's Worth
Brodie's Promise
Maddox's Truce
Naughton's Secret
Mercer's Vow
Kade's Return
Butler Ranch Christmas

WICKED WINEMAKERS
CENTRAL COAST
FIRST LABEL
Brix's Bid
Ridge's Release
Press' Passion
Zin's Sins
Tryst's Temptation

WICKED WINEMAKERS
CENTRAL COAST
SECOND LABEL
Beau's Beloved
Cru's Crush
Bit's Bliss
Snapper's Seduction
Kick's Kiss

WICKED WINEMAKERS
RUSSIAN RIVER VALLEY
FIRST LABEL
Bas' Blend
Hux's Harvest
Wolf's Want
Oak's Vintage
Cooper's Claim

COWBOY ROMANCE

COWBOYS OF
CRESTED BUTTE
A Cowboy Falls
A Cowboy's Dance
A Cowboy's Kiss
A Cowboy Stays
A Cowboy Wins

ROARING FORK RANCH
Roaring Fork Wrangler
Roaring Fork Roughstock
Roaring Fork Rockstar
Roaring Fork Rooker
Roaring Fork Bridger

SANGRE VISTA RANCH
Thorn's Stand
Stetson's Storm
Maverick's Reckoning
Cinch's Wager
Flints Chance

www.ingramcontent.com/pod-product-compliance
Lightning Source LLC
Chambersburg PA
CBHW060451300726
48975CB00008B/2468